Caught Up
IN HIS
Savage Ways

D'NISE COLLINS

Azia

"Azia, when you come in the house, you take those shoes off."

I had just walked through the door, and before I could do anything, she started going in on me. My mom had a severe case of OCD. Everything had to be in order, from her shoes to the food in the fridge. If it wasn't, she would run her mouth for hours at a time. I loved my mother, and I could never do any wrong in her eyes.

I grew up in the projects around a bunch of drug dealers and prostitution, but my mother worked long hours and overtime to move us out. When we finally moved, my mom bought us a house, and we never looked back.

We moved to the west side of Chicago, and it was very peaceful. I finished school, and my mom got a better paying job at a hospital close to our home. Three years ago, I graduated from high school. For two years, I had been a student at Moraine Valley community college, and I would soon graduate. Being an only child, my mom and grandma would take me on trips every summer, and I loved to fly. Those experiences as a little girl inspired me to become a flight attendant. Now, I was just waiting to get a call back from the airline to start my career.

When my grandma passed away from a heart attack, many things changed with my mom. She started working more hours to keep busy and avoid the pain of her loss. My mother had never drunk wine in her life, but she started drinking wine every weekend.

"Yes, I was about to, but you started going off. Who made you mad?"

"I'm not mad, Azia. I'm cooking dinner."

"What we eating tonight? I'm starving."

"Roast and potatoes, mac and cheese, and cornbread. Something simple."

"Sounds good to me. I'm going to get in the shower. I'm tired from school. Thank God I'll be done in two months."

"I'm proud of you, baby girl. You did an awesome job, and it will be worth it in the end."

"Thanks, Ma!"

I went upstairs to start the shower and get my pajamas ready. In June, I would be twenty-two, and I needed my own space, so I was looking for an apartment. Working and going to school was draining, but I had stacked my money, and now I was ready to leave the nest. I didn't have many friends; everyone was kind of weird to me. I did have one friend, though, and she would go to war about me and vice versa. Kameila was my homie. She had been down with me since I moved west six years ago, and the females in my neighborhood tried to fight me. According to the rumors, I think I'm better than everyone because, basically, I mind my own business.

After I got out of the shower, I slipped my pajamas on and went back to the kitchen to see if my mom was finished with dinner.

"I was wondering if you were ever going to come back downstairs," my mom said and giggled.

She must've had some wine.

"You know I'm not missing any meals, especially if you're the cook." I sat down at the table and started eating. "Mom, how is work going?"

"It's been going better ever since I became the manager. All the shifts are running smoothly, and everyone likes me."

"That's good. You know, we should take a trip some-where like old times. I think you and I need a vacation," I said.

"That sounds lovely, baby, but I don't know."

"Mom, it'll be great, and we'll have lots of fun. Grandma would love for us to still travel and live life."

"If you find somewhere to go, I'll go with you," she relented.

"It's going to be fun! You won't regret it."

My mother smiled, and we finished eating our food. She

hadn't been on a plane in years, and we both needed this vacation.

After dinner, I helped my mom clean the kitchen before going back to my bedroom. I pulled out my laptop and started looking for flights to Myrtle Beach. The flights were cheap, and we could leave in two days. My mom was on board with the plans, so we were good to go. I was so excited, like this was my first time on an airplane. When I texted Kameila and told her the details, she wanted to bring her mom, and I agreed. My mom and her mom were cool, so what harm could that do?

I turned the TV to LMN, and a movie was just starting. Lifetime has the best movies; I barely want to go to the bathroom when I'm watching. I would soon be asleep, though, because that shower and food had me in my happy place.

Soon as I was about to put my phone down, I got a message from this dude named Symon on messenger. We'd been talking a little through Facebook, but I wouldn't give him my actual number just yet. I wrote him back and was asleep before I knew it.

D'Metrius

"Yo, what up, bro? You heard what happened to that nigga Wyatt?"

I had called my nigga Punch to see if he heard the news. That nigga Wyatt got Fed time for getting caught with eight kilos of heroin. Wyatt was my connection to the game, and now that he was caught up, I had to find someone else. These niggas were too careless for me; I needed to make my own shit. I was known for having some pure ass shit, and I didn't want to get stuck with no damn bullshit. Punch and I were some hitters in these streets; nobody fucked with us. Everyone spoke to us, and most importantly, everyone shopped with us.

"Hell yeah, man, that's fucked up. Now what we gon' do, bro?"

"I still got some shit left, but we definitely gon' need some more soon."

"Fuck, man, somebody had to snitch on this nigga. He was always careful, from what we knew, anyway."

"Yeah, man, same shit I said."

I hung up with Punch and started thinking of a plan. There was no way I could be out here dry as fuck; these crackheads would be on my head, and I hated disappointing people. They wanted their hit, and I felt like I had to supply that shit.

I went downstairs and checked the stash to see what was left. We had enough for a couple more days, then we would need some more. I would have to call my uncle to see if he could hook me up with his plug for now. The only thing is, that nigga was in Miami, so I'd have to get on a plane and drive back. At that point, I was down for anything, though. I knew how to get my shit back without any problems. Shit, I had taken too many trips and was just fine. As long as I didn't speed, I would be good.

"Unc, I need you."

"Two days. Get on a plane, and I'll meet you at the airport," he said and hung up.

I already knew that would be the outcome. Unc knew I made money in these streets. That just ran through the family. My pops died in the streets, and I wasn't trying to be like that, but this fast money was important to me. I didn't have to ask a muthafuckin' soul for shit, and that was how I wanted to keep it. I called Punch back, and of course, my nigga was always down to take a trip.

I needed to make a sale, so I had to dip for a minute.

After a quick shower, I threw on some jeans and a t-shirt with my J's and was out the door. My sale wasn't far from my sister Meka's house, so I decided to make a pit stop just to check on her. She was twenty-two, working, and loved to have fun. I couldn't have my sister out there bold, so I showed her how to shoot at the age of sixteen. Once she got old enough, she got her license to shoot a muthafucka if they act stupid.

"Hey, bro, where are you coming from?" Meka asked when she opened the door.

"Handling some business. What are you about to do?"

"Head out to work. Somebody called off, and they asked me to cover for them. You know I love overtime."

"Yo' ass better be careful working at that damn club. I'm glad you got your pistol. People are weird nowadays, sis."

"Yeah, I know, but them niggas don't try me. They know who my brothers are."

"They already know me and Punch not for no games."

"Exactly. You talked to Mama lately? I've been trying her cell all day and haven't gotten an answer."

"I was about to ask you the same thing. I'm gon' stop by her house when I leave here. Try calling her job."

I left my sister and went to my mother's house. She always answered her phone or called us back. I had called her phone almost an hour ago, and she still hadn't called me back. When I pulled into her driveway, I noticed her car wasn't there, but I had a key. I needed to check her cameras and see when she had last been home. My mom was a manager at the airport, and she always worked long hours.

I walked into the house, and everything looked cool, so I went to the den and checked her cameras. I saw my mom walk into the house and go upstairs. A few minutes later, she came back down, grabbed her purse, and left right back out. She got in her car and drove off. That was four hours ago. Something wasn't right, and I needed to figure some shit out.

I called my sister back, and she answered on the first ring.

"Aye, what did her job say?"

"I talked to her manager, and she said they're not allowed to have phones on the floor, but she'll have Mama call me back."

"Alright, cool, 'cause I was about to tear the city up."

"Alright, crazy. Be careful. Love you."

"Love you too, sis."

I grabbed some food and went home. It was a slow day, so I was about to chill and get this bag packed for Miami. I walked into the house, and sitting on my couch was my ex-girlfriend, Cierra. I just shook my head because this girl was crazy, and I didn't even know how she got in there.

I set my food down, took my jacket off, and walked into the kitchen. By the time I washed my hands and came back out, Cierra was naked as the day she came out of her mama's pussy. This was about to be a long night. I could already tell.

"Cierra, why the hell are you naked?"

"You know you miss me, baby. Come get some of this."

"I'm straight. You can put your clothes back on. I'm tired, and yo' ass about to leave. How ever the hell you got in here, don't try that shit again."

"Why are you treating me like this?"

"I'm not answering questions today. Leave my house."

"Alright, fuck you then, Metri. Don't call my phone either."

She grabbed her shoes and walked out the door. I closed it behind her and turned on the TV. Tonight, I didn't have time for any bullshit.

Azia

"**M**om, it's time to get up for the trip. We have literally an hour to get to the airport."

"Alright, I'm up, I'm up."

I went back into my bedroom and started grabbing my things, so I could get in the shower really quick. The airport wasn't far from our house, so that was a good thing. After hopping in the shower, I hurried to put my clothes on. Finally, I grabbed my bag and met my mama in the living room. We grabbed our luggage and were out the door.

During the drive to the airport, my mom prayed for us to have a safe flight, and that eased her mind a lot. We made it five minutes before the flight boarding announcement. As we hurried to the gate, this guy bumped into me, and my ticket went flying across the floor. There were so many people walking around, and I got irritated because we were already late.

"My bad. I was trying to get out the way of this lady, and I didn't see you. Here's your ticket."

This fine ass guy was talking to me, and I was mesmerized for a second. He had a pretty smile with deep dimples. I figured he was probably in his early twenties, like me. My mind was so caught up in admiring his looks that I barely heard what he said.

"It's okay. We are all rushing. I was late myself," I said before grabbing the ticket and walking with my mom to the line. I couldn't stop smelling that cologne.

My heart started to beat fast as hell when I saw that the handsome stranger was getting on the same plane as us. My mom asked me if I was okay, and I nodded yes. Once we got on the plane, I found my seat and put my luggage up. I sat down and placed my pillow around my neck; my mom did the same.

"What were you and that guy talking about? You know he bumped into you on purpose, right?"

"He did not. We were all rushing, so it's no big deal, lady. You got your movies ready?"

"Yes, I do, and don't try to hush me up."

"I'm not. All he said was he apologize, and he was rushing."

"You like him, 'cause you keep smiling when you talk about him."

"I don't even know that dude. The plane is about to pull off, so put your AirPods in."

I had to shut her up because she would ask questions

the whole way, and I wasn't trying to hear that. The flight was only two hours, but we had one stop in Miami. I was ready to get in the shower and put on my swimsuit. While my mom closed her eyes, I started watching a movie.

When the airplane stopped for the others to get off in Miami, I saw that guy grab his belongings and leave. Finally, we made it to South Carolina and picked up our rental car before heading to the hotel.

"Hello, I have a reservation for Azia Cook," I said when we reached the hotel front desk.

"Okay, let me check that for you. I'll need your credit card and ID."

After checking in, we went to our rooms and changed into beach attire. Since we had connecting rooms, we just left the door open between them. Within twenty minutes, we were at the hotel bar near the beach.

"I need a margarita. School and work have been getting on my last nerves," I told my mom.

"I agree. Work has been getting on my nerves, too," my mom said.

"All you drink is wine. You sure you're ready for a margarita?" I laughed.

"We are on vacation, right? Let's live a little."

"Alright, let's get it, lady."

We got the drinks and went to the beach. For a while, we just stood on the sand and let our feet get wet. I felt an overwhelming sense of peace as I looked at the beautiful trees and the sun. The water was a pretty blue, and the sand was so soft. This was the type of scenery that I liked to wake up to. Eating on the patio and just enjoying the sun with my kids and husband. One day my dream would come true, and my mom would be right by my side to witness it all.

"How you feeling? You had two margaritas already," I asked my mother.

"I feel great, and this drink is good." She started dancing in a circle, and I just smiled. I missed her being like this, bubbly and fun.

"I'm getting hungry. Want to get changed and get something to eat?"

"That sounds like a plan."

We went back to the room and got changed. Since we both wanted seafood, I looked up the address of this one seafood place that I had read about on Facebook. It was twenty minutes from the hotel, and we had to park a block away. I read online that it was the best place in town, so I wanted to try it. The line was moving kind of fast, so that was good.

"Welcome to the best seafood place in town. How may I help you?"

"Yes, I want two seafood bags with crab legs, lobster tails, and shrimp."

"Okay. Would you like them regular, mild, or spicy?"

"One regular and one spicy."

"Okay, your total is 124.67."

The restaurant had so many customers, and the food smelled amazing. I scrolled through social media, but there was nothing interesting on there. As I scrolled, Kameila called. I wish she could've come, but she had to work the weekend, and this was short notice. My mom grabbed the food, and we went to the car, so we could return to the hotel and eat peacefully in our room.

"Hey, girl," I answered.

"Hey, boo. What are y'all doing?" Kameila asked.

"Me and Mama just got some seafood, and now we're on the way back to the room. What are you doing?"

"Girl, just got off work. I'm about to shower and go out to eat with Jerome's irritating ass."

"He wants that old thang back," I said, and we laughed.

"I don't want his ass back, but I don't feel like cooking, so I'll take the free meal."

"I know that's right."

We talked some more, then she needed to get ready for her date, so we hung up.

Once we got back to the hotel, I showered and slipped on my pajamas. I peeked in my mother's room, and she was knocked out. Happy that the first day of vacation was fantastic, I ate my food while watching a movie on Netflix.

D'Metrius

"Aye, ole girl was looking kind of good," Punch said as we pulled up to my uncle's home.

"Hell yeah. Shorty was thick and chocolate, just like I like it. I'm gon' get her name and find out what I need to know about her."

"I knew you were about to say that. That's why I brought her up!" He laughed.

"Shut yo' ass up and get serious. We about to walk in this nigga's crib."

"Nigga, I know."

As we walked up to my uncle's house, my heart pounded, probably because I knew this nigga was an asshole, and I didn't want to fuck shit up with my temper. Punch had a temper too, but I could control mine better. I let this let nigga know before we walked into the house, though!

"Let me forewarn you now that my uncle is an asshole. Just control yo' temper, bro. I know how we can get, but we only need this nigga for a couple of months. Once we get cool with his connect, we can cut this nigga out."

"I got you, bro."

My uncle was having a barbeque, and it was packed. He didn't mention anything about a party. I just wanted to get this info and be out. I wasn't the friendly type, and I couldn't be around too many niggas. My uncle was standing by the grill with an apron on. I shook my head and gave him a handshake. After I introduced Punch to him, he took us to his office.

"What up doe, nephew? How you been?"

"I've been good, just tryna get back to the paper. My old connect got caught up, and now he's doing time."

"So, you figured I would be the best resort?"

"I figured since we family, you could help me out. I got cash right now!"

"We family now, huh? You don't even text or call to check on me, but you want my help?" He looked confused, but his ass didn't call either.

"The phones work both ways, Unc. You don't call us. Look, we came here on some money getting shit, not no family matters." This nigga was pissing me off already.

"Yeah, alright. I called my connect, and he'll be here in a few minutes."

The nigga showed up ten minutes later. When he walked in, Unc made the introductions, but the nigga didn't even speak. He just sat in the chair and stared at me. I was about to say fuck this shit. These niggas were weird, and I didn't have time for the bullshit. I needed to get back to the city, so I could get some shit done.

"How many do you need?" Dhillon, the connect, finally asked.

"Look, I can start off with five and work my way up. This gon' sell in a few weeks, so I'll be back soon."

"Your uncle told me about you and how you like to get to the money. I'm gon' try you out with one. I'll give you five, and I want twenty percent."

"Bet. Let's do it."

I looked at Punch, and he was down with it. He already knew that with the money we were about to make, twenty percent ain't shit. We packed up the truck that my uncle gave me and headed back to the hotel to grab our things.

The hotel was thirty minutes away, but I made it in twenty. We were gon' be on the road for some hours, so I needed a nap. Punch went to his room, and I walked to mine. I was ready to get back home, so I could get this shit on the floor. I ordered some room service and watched football.

A few hours later, I went to get Punch, so we could head on out. I was surprised the meeting went well, and my uncle didn't put his two cents in.

"We on, bro. This is about to be a new start for us," Punch said.

"Yeah, bro, this shit pure too. You can look at the color and tell."

"Man, Tyesha keeps calling me. She's about to get blocked, bro."

"That's yo' girl. You can't block her." I laughed.

"Nigga, fuck you!"

Tyesha really wasn't his girl; he just fucked her a couple times, and she hadn't left his side. She was more like a security guard. Tyesha had people following Punch, and from time to time, she would pop up at his house. He had to get a restraining order on her, and that didn't help either. I told him to let my sister beat her ass one good time, but he didn't want to put Meka through any drama, so he said he'd deal with her himself.

"You ready to get on this road, my guy?" I said.

"Let's do it!"

We had a long drive, but in the end, it would be well worth it. Punch drove first while I took a nap, and then I drove the other half. My mind kept going back to that girl I ran into at the airport. Shorty was looking good, and I was determined to see her again. She had to live in Chicago because we were at the same airport... At least, I hoped that was the case.

Azia

Three Months Later

"*S*is, are you ready for tonight?"

"You know I am. I'm finally out of school, and I got the job I've always wanted."

"Yes, girl, and I'm so proud of you. You deserve everything good that's coming your way."

Kameila was always emotional. She hugged me, and it felt so good. This girl was like the sister I've always wanted. We were going to Club Lynx to celebrate, and I heard it be doin' numbers on Saturdays. Since I graduated last month and finally got the job as a flight attendant, I was so happy, and I just wanted to let loose for a night.

"I wanted to let you know that I invited a friend from school," I told Kameila.

"Girl, here you go! If she acts like a stuck-up bitch, I'm punching her ass."

"It will not come to that, sis. She's cool and not stuck up."

"Where is she meeting us? What's her name?"

"Her name is Rahna, and she's meeting us at the club."

It took us twenty more minutes to put the finishing touches on our hair. I wasn't really into make-up, but I put some on tonight. The club wasn't far, and we were already buzzing. This was going to be a great night. When we pulled up to the club, it was packed. There wasn't a long line, so I was cool with that. We hopped out as Rahna walked up to the car.

"Hey, girl."

"Hey, Rahna. This is my best friend, Kameila."

"Hey, love."

"Hey, girl, it's nice to meet you."

Kameila wasn't as rude as she seemed; she just didn't like new people. She never hung with the girls on our block because they were too stuck-up for her. I didn't care for those hoes either. They portrayed a good life, but behind closed doors, it wasn't so nice. I tried hanging with two of them, but I couldn't. They were drama-filled, and I was focused on my future.

"Y'all ready to have some fun and shake some asssss?" Kameila yelled, and we laughed.

"Hell, yeah. I need this night. Let's go, ladies," Rahna said.

We walked to the door, paid our twenty dollars, and headed straight to the bar. Once we got our drinks, I saw an empty table in the back, so I decided to grab it before someone beat us to it. It didn't have a reserved sign, so I figured it was cool. The club was packed, and those people weren't lames. They were on the dance floor, getting it in.

"This bitch is packed. I might find a baby daddy in here," Kameila said, and I laughed. Her ass was crazy.

"Bitch, your ass doesn't even want no kids, sis," I reminded her.

We had been sitting at the table for about two hours, talking shit and going on the dance floor, doing all the hustles. Since we all had on dresses, we weren't shaking that much ass tonight. My phone fell out of my hand, so I bent down to pick it up. When I looked back up, the guy from the airport was standing in front of me.

"What's up? Aren't you the girl from the airport?"

"Yes." I kept it short and simple.

"You know you're sitting at my table, right?" He licked his lips, and I had to catch my smile from forming.

"This is your table? It didn't have a sign saying it was yours."

"The manager was gon' come over here and tell you to leave the table. I'm just the messenger because I sort of know who you are."

"Well, my bad. We'll sit at the bar. I'm getting ready to leave in a minute anyway."

I grabbed my purse and was about to walk off when he grabbed my arm.

Kameila ran up fast as hell, and Rahna was right behind her. We didn't play about each other, and since she'd never actually seen the guy from the airport, Kameila didn't know who he was.

"It's cool, sis. This is the guy I was telling you about from the airport."

"Okay, but he can let your arm go. That's not how you get anybody's attention."

"You right, shorty. My fault. I was saying that y'all can stay here. It's cool."

Kameila looked at me, and I just told her it was a long story, and it was fine. We sat down, and some more guys showed up. They were all cute and buff. Nobody in this crew was ugly, and I could see my girls getting happy that it was some fresh dick in the booth.

D'Metrius

"Who are you over there texting, smiling and shit?" I asked my sister.

"Why are you all in my phone? You don't pay any bills this way."

"I just asked a question. Why are you getting so defensive?"

My sister had cooked dinner and invited my mother and me over. We were sitting at the dining room table enjoying a meal together. Things had been going well lately. We were making good money off this new connect, but my uncle was acting like a bitch, trying to take more profits because he saw that we were getting to the money and didn't play about this shit. I told that nigga it wasn't going to happen, though. He was probably about to be on some hoe shit, and I was gon' have to kill his ass.

"So, what are we doing for Christmas this year?" my mom asked.

"Whatever you want to do is fine with me," I said. I really didn't care about the holidays, but my mother and sister did.

"Ouu, we should go to a cabin and get away for that weekend."

"Sounds good to me. Look up the info and give it to me."

"Okay. This is going to be fun."

Crack!

We all jumped up and ran to the living room to see what happened. The front window was broken, and glass was all over the couch and floor. Now, who the fuck was breaking windows at my sister's crib? My eyes landed on Meka, and she just started looking around. She knew who did this, and she knew I was going to fuck them up.

"Who the fuck did this?"

"I don't know. I was in the dining room with you."

"Are you into it with someone, Meka?" my mom asked.

"No, I don't know who did this. All I know is I need this window fixed. I can't sleep with it broken."

I made a few calls, and the man was there within an hour to fix the window. Meka was going to stay at our mother's house tonight because I was gon' figure out who the fuck did this shit. It better not have been one of them dumb ass niggas she fucked with either. I called Punch and told him to pull up to her crib because we had some moves to make.

"What up, nigga? What happened?" Punch asked when he got to Meka's place.

"We were sitting in the dining room eating and shit, and next thing you know, we heard glass shatter."

"What the fuck! Does she know who it was?"

"Man, I don't know, but we gon' find out. The streets talk too damn much."

"That's the truth, bro. Let's ride."

We rode around for an hour, but nobody seemed to be in the streets. It was only a matter of time before we found out what happened, though. I wasn't tripping because the window got fixed, but somebody was gon' pay for it, and not with money.

My phone rang, and it was this chick named Honei. I had been fucking with her for a year, but she wasn't what I wanted, and I was trying to get rid of her ass.

"What up?" I answered.

"Hey, bae, what are you doing?"

"What did I tell you about calling me that? I'm not doing shit but chilling. Why?"

"I wanted to come over tonight and cook you dinner. Can that happen?"

"Yeah, that's cool. I'll call you when I get home."

I hung up the phone before she started saying that *I love you* shit. Although I liked her cooking, and she had some bomb ass pussy, that shit wasn't all I needed in a relationship. I needed stability, loyalty, growth, and love. Honei always wanted to argue, and I got tired of that shit. She had slashed my tires before and even stalked me out of town but tried to act like she was there for business. Honei was a lawyer, and at thirty-one, she was older than me but acted childish as hell.

"Are you going home, bro?" Punch asked.

"Naw, I got to get my truck from Meka's crib."

He dropped me off at my truck, and I went home. I got in the shower and turned on a football game while I rolled a blunt. When I called Honei, she must've been on the corner because she showed up two minutes after I hung up.

While Honei went into the kitchen and started cooking, I smoked my blunt. She wanted us to have kids, but she wasn't the person I wanted to have kids with. Honei would have to change a lot of things before that could happen.

My phone rang just as I finished rolling my blunt.

"Metri, you have to get to Mama's house. She just had a heart attack!"

"What? I'm on the way!" I sprinted into the kitchen. "Aye, you gotta go. Cut the stove off, and I'll drop you off back at home. I have an emergency."

I rushed to put on my shirt and shoes. Honei was looking stupid, but I didn't have time to explain. I literally pulled her by her arm because she was moving slow. After I dropped her off, I rushed to my mama's house, just to see the ambulance leaving with her. My sister was gone, so I figured she must've been in the ambulance with her. I hopped in my car and sped to the hospital; I damn near beat them here.

"What happened?" I asked Meka.

"I walked into the living room, and she was just sitting on the couch. I started talking to her, and she didn't respond. So, I walked over to her and was like, 'Ma, why you not answering me?' I saw that her eyes were turning a different color, so I got scared and called 911."

"Fuck, man, I hope she's good. I can't lose my mama."

"Me either, bro."

I paced the floor while we waited for answers. This was the first time this had ever happened, and I was scared. I called Punch and let him know what happened, so he could take care of business for a couple of hours. I thought about texting Azia just to take my mind off this shit, but I decided against it and sat next to Meka. I had gotten her number before she left the club that night, and we had been talking ever since. She was cool, and I looked forward to getting to know her.

"Family of Sherry Mags," I heard the doctor say, and we jumped up.

"Yes, is our mother okay? When can we see her?" Meka started asking questions.

"I'm sorry. She didn't make it. Her arteries had a blockage, and her heart wasn't getting enough blood. She never mentioned any of this to you guys?"

"No. As far as we knew, she was healthy."

"No, sir, she has been a patient here for the past month. How about we go to the back and talk?"

Man, I was so fucking hurt, and I didn't know what to

do. It was just sis and me now, and I'd be damned if I lost her too. We had some shit to talk about, and some things were about to change. I couldn't believe my mother had coronary artery disease and didn't tell us anything. The day we were looking for her, she was in the hospital getting all these treatments and taking all kinds of tests.

My head started hurting, and I just wanted to get home. I told Meka she was coming to my house. She just shrugged and got in the car. We both were so hurt, and I needed my sister, so she wasn't going back home just yet.

"You don't know me, but I just wanted to say I'm sorry for your loss." One of the nurses came up to me, and she looked familiar, but I just said thank you and walked out the door.

Meka

It was the day of my mother's funeral and the first day that I had gotten out of bed since she passed. I just couldn't believe my mother was gone. She had that disease for a whole year and didn't tell us anything. Metri and I were so hurt when we found out. We weren't surprised, though, because she was always good at keeping secrets.

My eyes filled with fresh tears as I looked at my outfit in the mirror. I decided to wear a black skirt and a nice blouse with some flats. I couldn't wear heels all day because I would get irritated when my feet started killing me. When I walked down the stairs, Key, my best friend of ten years, was sitting on the couch. I was so surprised because she had been in New York for the last two months.

"When I talked to you, you didn't say you were coming home," I said as I hugged her.

"I know you don't like surprises, but I had to. You know I love Mama Sherry!"

"Yeah, I know. Key, it's just crazy."

"Y'all two ready? The car is outside for us," Metri walked in and said.

"Yes, let me grab my purse."

When we pulled up to the funeral home, I couldn't make myself get out of the car. The reality of the situation had just hit me like a ton of bricks.

I looked at my brother, and he said, "Come on, sis. This is hard for both of us, but you know I got you."

When he said that, I felt a chill. I knew he was right; my brother always had my back. We may argue and not speak for a few days, but I could always count on him and vice versa.

My mother still looked beautiful, even in her casket. The funeral lasted an hour, then we went to the cemetery for the burial.

"Best friend, I got your back, and you know we'll always be here for you," my bestie said as she held my arm.

"Yes, I know. Let's go get some food. I'm starving."

"I made a reservation at Betty's Soul Food," Metri announced.

"Ooou, bro, that's the place right there."

We drove twenty minutes to the restaurant, and it was packed. I kind of figured it would be since it was a Sunday, and everyone went there after church. So glad my brother made reservations for us and some of the family that came back with us. It was bittersweet to sit at the table, knowing my mother wouldn't be able to join us.

"I remember when we were kids, and your mother ran outside to get the ice cream truck. She fell as soon as she hit the curb. Me and your grandma went outside, and she had a big gash on her knee. The ice cream man came out of his truck and gave her three ice creams. She was happy for that whole day, hurt knee and all," my cousin Jill said.

"Aww, she still had that scar on her knee, but I never asked her about it," I responded.

I looked at Metri, and he was smiling while texting somebody on his phone. Punch was there, and he looked good as hell. I couldn't touch him, though, but I damn sure wanted to. My brother would probably kick my ass. Plus, Punch thought of me as his sister. But damn, he was fine. Punch was brown-skinned with deep ass waves, a pretty smile, and he was buff. He always dressed nicely and always smelled good. He was a few years older than me, but I didn't care.

"Who are you over there texting, bro?"

"This lil' chick I met at the airport like three months ago."

"You're not gonna' eat your food?" Key asked.

The face he made caused her to look down at her phone, and she didn't look back up.

"Why are you looking at Key like that, Metri?" I had to know.

"I just don't feel like talking."

"But you over there texting," she pointed out.

"Don't worry about me. Plus, texting is not talking."

When Metri got in his moods, everyone knew to leave his ass alone. Eventually, he would come around. No one really felt like talking, so the table was pretty quiet as we ate our food.

When I finally made it home, I couldn't wait to jump in the shower. Key had gone back home since she hadn't seen her mom at all today. Noticing a text message from Lucus brought a smile to my face. I met him at the club while I was bartending two weeks ago. He was so sweet; he literally stayed at the bar with me until my shift was over. He didn't have a girlfriend or any kids. Until he showed me otherwise, I didn't mind kicking it with him from time to time.

Lucus: Hey beautiful, what are you doing?

Me: I just got in the house from my mother's funeral and eating.

Lucus: I'm so sorry to hear that. Do you feel like talking?

Me: I was about to lie down and watch a movie. I'm just in my feelings right now!

Lucus: That's understandable. Text me tomorrow, beautiful, and have a great night.

Me: I will, and thank you!

See, that's what I'm talking about. He was so sweet and thoughtful of my feelings. I was kind of scared to get into another relationship, though. My ex-boyfriend, Ty, was a maniac, and he was the one who broke my window that night. I hadn't told my brother yet because I didn't want him to get in any trouble behind killing a nigga. We had just lost our mother, and I'd be damned if I lost him too.

Knock! Knock! Knock!

"Now, who could be at my door?" I mumbled as I got up and headed to the living room. "Who is it?" I asked.

"Open the door, bae."

"Ty, why are you here?"

"Because I miss you, and I wanted to see you. I can't call or text because you blocked me."

"That should tell you something then. I don't want to be bothered right now."

"Come on, now. Open the door, please."

Against my better judgment, I opened the door. He stood there with a big ass teddy bear, some chocolates, and some roses. Ty was always sweet; I just couldn't take his temper when he got mad because he couldn't get his way.

I had just buried my mother, and I didn't want to be alone, but I didn't want to be with him either. With a sigh, I took the roses and placed them in the vase, then I took the chocolates and put them in the freezer. Finally, I turned on a movie, and we watched it until I fell asleep.

Azia

My excitement was at an all-time high as I packed for my first flight as an attendant. I was so excited because we were going to Miami. I couldn't wait to leave, and it was two days away. My cell phone went off, and it was D'Metrius. I smiled because we had been talking a lot more lately. He'd lost his mom a week ago, and I felt so bad. I couldn't imagine losing my mother; that lady was my world. He wanted to take me to dinner tonight, and I agreed. This would be our first date, and I couldn't stop smiling.

"Hey, baby, I'm on my way to work. I'll see you tonight when I get off," my mom stuck her head in my room and said.

"I probably won't be here when you get off, Mom. I have a date!"

"Oh, my god, I'm so happy for you. It's that boy Meechie or something, right?"

I laughed. "Yes, Mom, but his name is D'Metrius."

"Sounds the same to me. Have a great date, and call me."

"I will. I love you."

"I love you too, baby."

She left for work, and I continued packing. I also looked in the closet for something to wear tonight, but I found nothing at all. So, I called up my bestie and told her she had to come with me to the mall. I told her why, and she was down to ride. The mall was twenty minutes away, and it was a Saturday, so I really hoped it wasn't crowded. I really disliked driving, so I had Kameila drive.

Just like I thought, it was a damn crowd at the mall. "Girl, this mall is crowded. I think they're selling dope or something with these clothes."

"You a damn idiot," she said, and we laughed.

"So, what do you plan to wear? Some jeans, a dress, or what? Tell me something. We need to have this shit in order."

"I don't know. That's why I brought you along to help me out, Ms. Fashionista."

"I do know how to dress, don't I?"

"You're irri. Let's go do some shopping."

We got out of the car and headed into the mall for a day of shopping. I wasn't rich, but I had some money to spend, so we went into all the stores. The trick was, I had to get Kameila to go with me on the date. She was so picky with her guys and liked the hood niggas who sold drugs and shit. I wasn't into that type; I wanted someone to treat me nice, take me out, and send sweet little messages during the day, just to let me know he was thinking of me.

I needed someone with a legal job and making legal money. Drug money always caused a problem. I didn't want to get woken up out of my sleep with someone telling me my nigga died or he had been locked up. I didn't know what D'Metruis was into, but if it was dealing with drugs, I would be out.

"Why the hell are you daydreaming and not picking out anything?" Kameila asked.

I didn't even notice I had zoned out. "Girl, I was thinking about what to wear," I lied.

"Yeah, yeah, yeah! I think you should wear a dress and some nice heels."

"Okay, let's see what we can find."

After spending two hours in the mall, going from store to store, we finally left. I had talked Kameila into letting me buy her an outfit and some shoes. D'Metrius had texted me and told me to be ready by 7:30. So, I guessed it was time to ask her since I had already set this up. She was going to be upset, but she'd be fine.

"So, I was thinking, D'Metrius got a best friend, and I want you to come with me on this date."

"Bitch, I knew you were up to something. How does this friend look?"

I knew I had her then. "I don't know if you were paying

attention the night we went to the club. The guy who had on the blue shirt and walked over with Metri to *their* table."

"Nah, I'm gon' need a picture or something. I can't take one for the team this time. Furthermore, I don't remember any blue shirts." We laughed.

"See, that wasn't my fault. He lied about his looks, sis."

"Yeah, bitch, whatever. But you know I got your back. What time are we leaving?"

"Seven-thirty. You can just get ready at my house. My mom is at work."

"You just said that like we're teenagers and sneaking out of the house."

Kameila dropped me off at home and then left to get ready. It was already five o'clock. I ran some bathwater and turned the music on. It was a good thing I had braids, so all I had to do was put my hair in a cute bun or some type of up-do. I had found a black dress with some leopard print around the neck, arms, and bottom, which I paired with black wedges that also had leopard print on the straps. It was so cute, and I hoped I picked the right outfit.

After washing up and rinsing off in the shower, I grabbed my towel and got out. I stood in the mirror and fixed my hair three times before I decided on a simple bun. Finally, I put on my Bath and Body Works lotion then slid into my dress. As I stood in the mirror and admired my beauty, my phone went off with a text message.

D'Metrius: I hope you're ready because I'm outside.

Me: Yes, I am, and you're just on time.

I called Kameila, and she said she was pulling up. This night was about to be fun. I was excited about my first flight as an attendant, I was going on a date with this handsome guy, and my bestie would get to experience it with me. D'Metrius seemed nice, but I didn't want to go out with him on my own because I barely knew him, and we had talked maybe four times on the phone. I needed to see new faces and feel new vibes, so I was down to try almost anything once.

"Daammnn, you look fly as hell, bestie," Kameila said as she got out of her car.

"She ain't lying. You beautiful." D'Metrius came up to me and took my hand.

"Y'all got me blushing, but thanks. Kameila, you the one who looks fineee, bitch. I love that outfit."

"Yo, this my brother Wayne, but everybody calls him Punch."

"Ouuu, now where you get a name like that from, with your fine self?" Kameila said.

I just looked at her and shook my head.

"I'll tell you all about it at dinner, but reservations are at eight, so we got to go," Punch said.

"Cute and on time. I like him already."

We laughed and got in the truck. This was going to go smoothly; I could feel it. Kameila thought Punch was cute, and she was happy, so we'd see. The restaurant was thirty minutes away from my house, so we got there at a little after 8:00.

When we walked into the restaurant, I was impressed. It was beautiful, and the lobby had a wine bar and wine-themed gifts for sale. I even spotted a stand where they were selling little chocolate desserts. This place had to have some banging food and the finest wine. The restaurant's name was Cooper's Hawk, and I was ready to be seated because the food had it smelling so good. We were in the back by ourselves, and we had two waiters who only dealt with our table. Looking at the menu, I thought, *I hope he didn't forget his wallet,* and a laugh escaped.

"You found something funny looking at the menu?" D'Metrius asked.

"Yes, I did. These damn prices."

"You don't have anything to worry about. I got you."

The server came over and took our orders. We ordered two different wine flights and got to know each other while tasting different wines. It was really nice. I found out that D'Metrius had a sister, and she worked at the club he wanted to go to after dinner. I didn't really do clubs, but I would go out sometimes with Kameila when she asked. She and Wayne seemed to be hitting it off quite well, and I was so relieved.

"Did you enjoy your food?" D'Metrius asked.

"Yes, that salmon was so good, and they seasoned those shrimp very well."

"I'm glad you liked it. Are you ready to hit the club?"

"Yes, I am."

D'Metrius

I know y'all are probably wondering why I would take Azia to a club for a first date, but I had a drop to make, and the nigga was meeting me at the club. She and her girl would be at the table, so hopefully, no one would see them. This probably wasn't the best decision, but I wasn't ready for Azia to go home yet. Going to the club wasn't part of the original plan, but I had gotten a text while we were at the restaurant, and one of my regulars wanted a kilo. I wasn't about to miss that money, so I just asked her to come with me.

Punch was hitting it off with Kameila, so that was good. I could tell they weren't ready to go home, so why not go to the club with us?

"I hope y'all got a table, 'cause this damn club is crowded," Kameila said.

"You don't have to worry, baby. I always got a table," Punch replied.

"Okay, well, let's go inside."

That muthafucka was packed like somebody was having a party. Maybe that was why that nigga Rico wanted a kilo. We walked the ladies to the table and told them to order what they wanted. Azia wanted some wine, and Kameila ordered Hennessey. While they ordered, I texted Rico to see where he was.

Meka walked over to us and started talking shit. "Oouu, who are these pretty ladies, brothers?"

"This is Azia, my date, and that is Kameila, Punch's date," I introduced them.

"Hey, ladies, I'm Meka. These are my brothers, and I love them dearly, so please don't be no crazy-ass females."

They looked at each other and laughed.

"Girl, we are good over here. As long as they not no bitch niggas, you don't have nothing to worry about," Kameila said.

"Let me get back to work, but I like her, though." Meka smiled and walked away.

"Don't mind her ass. She's crazy," I said and chuckled.

"Trust me, I'm not worried," Azia responded.

I looked at my phone, and Rico had texted me to meet him in the back.

"Rico said to meet him in the back," I whispered to Punch

"Bet. Let's go."

I told Azia I would be right back, and she said okay, so I was trying to make it fast. I didn't know if Azia was aware of what was going on, but her friend didn't look like a rookie. She gave me that eye like, *nigga, I know what you doing.* I hoped she wouldn't open her mouth to Azia. One night, while we were talking on the phone, she told me that she didn't like drug dealers. I didn't plan to do this too much longer. This shit was a lot of work, and I was tired of watching my back because of these hating ass niggas.

Punch and I had almost made it to the back door when this chick named Ashley that I had been messing with stopped me and told me she wanted to see me tonight. I told her I'd come to find her after I was done with what I had to do.

"Yo, what took you so long?" Rico asked.

"I came when I got here. Where's my money?"

"Calm down, bro. I got your money right here."

He pulled out a gun and pointed it at me.

"Nigga, what the fuck you doing?"

"I want the kilo, but I don't have the money, so I'm taking it... got it?"

"Nigga, you know that's not about to happen."

Pow! Punch shot his ass. He didn't know Punch was standing by the back door. Niggas always trying to be slick. Now it was a dead body, and we had to get the fuck on. We went back to the booth, but the ladies were both gone. Azia didn't text me or anything. I called her phone while walking up to the bar to ask Meka if she saw where they went. She said they went outside and hadn't come back in yet. I looked outside, and she wasn't out there.

"Did you get Kameila's number?" I asked Punch.

"Hell naw, I didn't get it yet."

"Man, where the fuck could they be?"

"I don't know, bro, but we have to get the fuck on. They not here."

Punch was right, so we got in the car and went back to my house. I tried calling Azia three more times, and she didn't answer, so I just gave up. I couldn't believe this nigga had tried to kill me, and he was one of my regulars. He had to die for trying that dumb shit with me. Rico should've already known my dawg was gon' be right there.

Once I made it home, I got in the shower and turned on the basketball game. I tried calling Azia two more times with no luck. My cell phone rang, and I thought it was her, but it was Ashley.

"What's up?"

"How come you never came to find me at the club?" she asked.

"I had an emergency, so I had to go."

"Yeah, well, I'm glad you did. Somebody got shot in the back of the club."

"Damn, for real?"

"Yes, and the police were all up and through that place. I got the fuck on."

"Damn, that's fucked up."

"Can I come over tonight? I miss you."

"I'm really not feeling it tonight. I just want to sleep."

"You know what? Fuck this, you always on bullshit."

Click!

Ashley's little tantrum didn't faze me because I knew she'd be calling me tomorrow or texting me in a minute with some more bullshit. I turned my phone on do not disturb, even though I wasn't sleepy. I really wanted to know what Azia was up to and why she left the club without letting me know.

It was only a little after midnight, and I didn't know if Azia was awake, but I was on my way to her house. When I pulled up, I saw the same car that was there earlier, so I got out and walked up to the door. I knocked two times and waited for her to answer. A minute later, I heard footsteps, and that was a good sign.

"D'Metrius, why are you here?" Azia snapped when she opened the door.

"Damn, what did I do to deserve that tone?"

"I was lying down. What's up?"

"What's up? Why did you leave the club like that without letting me know you were gone?"

"Because you had other plans, and I didn't want to ruin them."

I looked at her crazy as hell. "What plans did I have?"

"When you left the table, I did too. I was going to the restroom when I heard your little friend ask you if she could come over. You said you were going to find her after you were finished. So, after I used the restroom, I went back to the table to get my friend, and we left."

Damn, I didn't even know she was behind me. That's why Ashley came up to me in the first place—because she saw me there with her. I was glad I turned her ass down tonight because she did too fucking much. Now I had to get back on good terms with Azia. I didn't know what to say, but she wasn't going anywhere that fast.

"That girl doesn't mean shit to me. She's just a friend."

"That's fine."

"What does that mean?"

"We're still friends. I can't get mad because you're not my boyfriend."

"You got mad because you're starting to like me. It's cool. I feel the same way."

"That's not going to work with me being a flight attendant now."

"Trust me, I'll find a way. It's getting cold out here, so answer your phone."

"I left my phone at the club. I have to get another one tomorrow."

"Here's my phone. I'll call it when I get to the house."

"No. What if somebody calls it?"

"You can answer it or not."

Azia looked at me crazy, but she took the phone anyway. Nobody called that phone but my mama and my sister. I only gave that number out to important people, and she had that number. I had another phone for the other girls and my trap phone. If everything went well, I would get rid of that second phone. I knew I could get Azia to fall in love with me; I just had to learn how to let these hoes go. I wasn't getting sex from Azia yet, so... I mean, I needed somebody to keep my dick wet.

Azia

I left my phone in the bathroom at the club last night and didn't realize it until I got home. After I overheard the conversation between D'Metrius and that chick, I just wanted to leave. I was starting to like him, and it bothered me that he talked to other girls. I couldn't be mad at him about that, so I brushed it off when he came to the house last night.

I honestly didn't know if he heard what she said. He was walking fast and looked like he was in a rush, so he just told her anything. When D'Metrius gave me his phone last night, I was surprised. That's the last thing I expected him to do. We talked for like two hours after he left, and I can say that when he becomes mine, he'll be mine forever.

"Good morning, baby girl," my mom greeted me when I walked into the kitchen.

"Good morning, Mom. How was work last night?"

"It was actually a great night. Nothing out of the norm."

"That's good. Where are you on your way to this morning?"

"I offered to take the morning shift today, so I can get off early."

"Okay. I have to get a new phone. I lost mine yesterday."

"I was wondering what happened. I called you three times last night."

"I was hanging with Kameila, and I left my phone in the bathroom at the club."

"That's a story for later because it sounds like I'm going to need some wine."

I laughed and gave my mom a hug before she left. She had made breakfast, and I was hungry. I was still kind of buzzing from those drinks. My mom made waffles, eggs, bacon, and grits. Eager to dig in, I grabbed a plate and poured some orange juice.

I heard the phone ringing that D'Metrius gave me last night, so I went upstairs to answer it. I thought it was him, but it was his sister, so I ignored it and went back downstairs to finish eating.

Breakfast was delicious, and I was now energized and ready to take on the day. After washing the dishes, I got in the shower and put my clothes on. Today would be a busy one; I had to finish getting the things I needed for work and purchase a new phone. I got to the door, and as soon as I opened it, I spotted D'Metrius standing next to my car, holding some flowers.

"This is so sweet. Thank you!"

"You're welcome, beautiful. I also got you this." He handed me a phone box.

"You bought me a new phone too? You didn't have to do this." I smiled.

"Listen, it was kind of my fault that you left your other phone at the club. I decided to get another one for you. It's no big deal, baby."

His voice was making me wet!

"Thank you again. I appreciate it." I gave him a hug for the first time. His body was so strong, and I didn't want to let go.

"How about you ride with me today?"

"I have to get some things for work tomorrow. You know I'm going on my first flight as an attendant."

"Yes, I know. Where do you have to go?"

"Just to Walmart."

"We can stop by there. I'll take you."

"Okay, cool. Let me grab my purse."

I didn't know what I had agreed to, but the damage was already done. Demetrius was just so sweet. I knew this was how everything started off, so I wasn't going to get too carried away. At the same time, I hadn't felt this way in a long time, and it felt good to be wanted again.

I grabbed my purse and locked the door. D'Metrius was driving a truck today, so I figured he was in Wayne's car yesterday. The truck was clean, and it smelled so good. Our first stop was Walmart. I needed some snacks, water, and other little things.

"How long will you be gone?" D'Metrius asked.

"I'll be working for sixteen hours tomorrow. With me being new, I'm on call and have to make my schedule flexible."

"Sounds like you can't wait for tomorrow."

"I really can't. This is what I've always wanted since I was a little girl. My grandma and mother used to take me on trips almost every summer until my grandma died. When I first saw you at the airport, that was me and my mother's first time getting back on a plane since she passed."

"I'm sorry to hear that, but I'm glad you're following your dreams, beautiful. A lot of people don't do that."

"You only live once. Better to say you did it than to say you wanted to but never got the chance."

"Facts!"

We laughed and grabbed everything I needed for my job. I was smiling because I felt like a little kid. Butterflies filled my stomach just from him holding my hand, and I wondered what this relationship would be like. I still hadn't asked him what he did for a living and wasn't sure I really wanted to know. I kind of thought he dealt with illegal activities, but I hoped not.

After D'Metrius paid for my stuff, he wanted to get some food, so we went to a burger spot and carried it out. As we waited for our food, he got a call and had to go somewhere to help his sister.

"What the is fuck going on?" D'Metrius spat as soon as he pulled up to his sister's house, where she was waiting for him on the porch.

"This guy came up to me before I could get in the house. He asked me if I knew where you were. I asked him who he was, and he said to tell you an old friend is looking for you. I've never seen him before, Metri, so who is he?"

"I don't know who the hell he is. What did he look like?"

"He had a mask on, and he was holding a gun by his side."

"Man, what the fuck is really going on? You are staying at my house tonight, so pack a bag," D'Metrius demanded.

"But I don't want to go to your house. I got protection, bro. I didn't call you because I was scared; I called because I need you to be on your shit."

"I feel that, and I know you good, but one nigga can turn into three. I'm not with that, so pack a bag and go to my house."

Meka huffed and went into the house.

I stared at D'Metrius, waiting for an explanation. This shit was crazy, and I didn't want to become a victim of anyone's bullshit. After a few minutes, Meka came back out, carrying a bag, and got in her car.

Once she left, D'Metrius took me back home, and the whole ride was quiet. I wanted to see if he would tell me what was going on, but he said nothing. We pulled up in front of my house, and he turned the car off. D'Metrius sat leaned over in the seat toward the window, rubbing his beard as he studied me. He looked so sexy, too, but that wasn't gon' cut it.

"So, you're not gonna tell me what's going on?" I asked.

"I can't tell you something I don't know."

"What are you into that has random guys looking for you?"

"I'm not into anything. I don't know what's going on, but I'm going to figure it out."

"Okay. Thank you for buying my things and bringing me home."

"You know I got you, shorty. I'm gon' call you in a minute."

He got out and opened my door, then gave me a hug. I stared up into his eyes, trying to see if I could read his truth before I pulled away and walked to my door. Once I had the door unlocked, D'Metrius got in his car and pulled off.

I had to be at work by six in the morning, so I made sure my bag was packed before changing into some sweats. I planned to relax for the rest of the day.

A few hours later, Kameila called me, and we talked for almost two hours. She told me that she and Wayne had been doing good, and she liked him. I was happy for my friend. She needed someone who would love her and treat her well.

What I had witnessed today with D'Metrius still weighed heavily on my mind. I didn't want to think about the possible adverse outcomes of this situation, so I hopped in the shower and got myself ready for my first day of work.

BEEP! Beep! Beep! Beep!

That was all I heard from this damn alarm clock. When I tried to go to sleep last night, it didn't work. I ended up falling asleep at 2:30 this morning. I had to be at work thirty minutes early, and I wasn't trying to be late. So, I took a quick shower since I already had my clothes out. Then, I woke my mom up and told her I was leaving and would call her as soon as possible. She said okay, told me she loved me, and that she would be waiting for my call. I loved her so much; I'd do anything to see her smiling again.

I grabbed a bagel and some coffee, then headed out to the car. I was glad I had upgraded and got an automatic start because this morning air was crazy cold. As I drove, I saw a car behind me, so I sped up a little and kept looking out the window. I made a right turn, and the vehicle did the same thing. Now, I was getting nervous. I pressed the gas and tried to get into the parking lot as fast as I could. After I parked, I hurried up and grabbed my things.

Once I got out of my car, I tried to look into the vehicle that was following me, but all I saw were two dudes that I didn't recognize.

"Good morning, Ms. Cook. How are you this morning?"

"Good morning, Mr. Jones. I'm doing great, just ready to get started." I smiled.

"Okay, well, just follow me, and I will show you around."

"Great!"

We walked down the hallway, and he showed me the airplane that I would be on. I still had an hour before we left. While waiting for the pilot to get there, Mr. Jones showed me the bathrooms, the food places, and the main office.

The pilot came about twenty minutes later, and I introduced myself. He looked like he was in his thirties. He wasn't super cute, but he wasn't super ugly either. I got on the plane, put my bag in the cubby, then went to use the restroom. My phone dinged with a text message.

D'Metrius: Good morning, beautiful. I hope you have a great day at work and call me when you can.

Me: Good morning, handsome, and thank you.

I tucked my phone away, and we waited for the passengers to get on the plane. It was mostly young people going to Miami. They were all coupled up, and it made me a bit wistful. I wanted to take a trip with my man one day, but I would have to see where things went with D'Metrius. One thing for sure, I wasn't willing to waste years with one man if he wasn't trying to make me his wife.

I called my mother and let her know I made it to work, and we were about to take off. She was at work and told me to call her as soon as I could. I also got a message from Kameila, telling me the same thing, and I texted her back.

A few minutes passed. "Ladies and gentlemen, the captain has turned on the fasten seatbelt sign. If you haven't done so already, please stow your carry-on luggage underneath the seat in front of you or in an overhead bin. Please take your seat and fasten your seatbelt," Mr. Lee, the lead flight attendant, announced.

As we took off, my heart overflowed with gratitude. *I was living my dream!* Once we reached cruising altitude, I eagerly went to the back to get the snack and drink cart.

Kameila

"*M*eila, you need to find a job and start paying some rent," my mother said when I walked into the living room.

"I'm looking for a job, Mom. It's not going to happen in three days."

"Well, these bills need to be paid, and I can't keep paying your half and mine."

"You know what? I didn't complain when I was the only one doing it at one point. I have been out of a job for one month, and you're already starting with me. That's why I didn't want to move back here anyway."

She was always starting bullshit with me whenever she couldn't get her way with her so-called boyfriend. I was tired of this shit, and I needed to find a way to get some money, so I could get the fuck on. Although I was looking for a job, people weren't really hiring like that. I was getting irritated with filling out these applications and not getting a call back.

My childhood wasn't that bad, but it wasn't good either. I used to get whoopings for anything. If she got mad at someone and couldn't get to them, she'd start something with me because she knew I had a smart mouth. She'd make that an excuse to whoop me or curse me out.

I went to live with my dad when I was fourteen, and it was great. I always got anything I wanted. He was a mail-man, and he loved his job. He barely missed a day unless he was sick and really couldn't go. One day I was at school, and my mom called and told me my dad was in a car accident. I left class and caught the bus to the hospital, crying the whole way. People were asking me if I was okay and if I needed help, but I couldn't talk. I was just ready to get to the hospital. My father died two minutes before I made it through the door.

"Girl, bye. I always helped. I'll tell you what... you can find some money or get out."

"Don't trip. I'll be gone soon."

I jumped in my car and went to see my friend Damon. His dad owned a few apartments, and I was about to see if I could pay to move right now. I had three thousand saved up from working, but my mom always blew her money and expected me to pay the bills. This time, I wasn't going for it, so I was ready to go. If Damon's dad couldn't help me, I would stay in a hotel and figure things out.

Luckily, he was at home because I didn't even think to call first.

"Hey, Damon, what's going on?" I said when he answered the door.

"Nothing, just chilling. What are you up to? Haven't seen you in a minute."

"I'm looking for an apartment. I can't continue to stay with Tammy. She's irritating as hell. I haven't been up to anything for real, but I'm thinking about selling my edibles again."

"You gon' start back making them? My birthday party is in two weeks, and I'll let you sell them there if you want."

"For real, D? That's so sweet. Yes, I'll buy all the stuff, and I'll be at your party. Can you do me this huge favor, please?"

"What's up?"

"Can you see if your dad has an apartment for rent? I need to move asap."

"It's a good thing he left me in charge. I actually have a two-bedroom for rent."

"Are you serious? That's good. Can I go look at it and sign the papers?"

"Yes, follow me."

I got in the car with a huge smile on my face; I was ready to move and have my own space. The house was twenty minutes from Damon's house, and it was in a nice neighborhood. There were kids outside riding their bikes, playing basketball, and playing hopscotch. It didn't seem bad at all, and I was ready to pack my bags. After he showed me around the house, Damon emailed me the lease, and I signed it through an app. The rent was just the right price, and I paid the first three months in advance.

Damon left, and I just walked around the apartment smiling. I finally had my own space and some peace.

My phone rang, and it was Wayne calling.

"Hello."

"What are you doing?"

"Nothing, about to leave my new apartment and get my things from this other house."

"Oh, word? Congratulations. You need some help moving your things in?" he asked.

"Look at you, being all helpful, but no, I got it this time. All I have are bags. I'll have my furniture delivered sometime this week," I told him.

"Okay, cool. I was just calling to check on you. Call me later or call me if you need anything."

"I sure will, Wayne. Thanks for checking on me."

Wayne was so sweet, and I knew he was into dealing drugs. I had gone with him to do a couple drops to his people who were running out of product. I was cool with the lifestyle because everybody doesn't grow up to be doctors and lawyers. They follow whatever path is available at that moment, is what I believe. I had been making edibles on and off for a year. Usually, I only made them when someone asked me to, but I had been thinking about making that my business. Once I got my marijuana license, I might just open a dispensary.

I liked decorating too; I had so many things I could do. Then again, I needed to start by going back to school, so I could get started on my career. I was so happy for Azia. She started her job yesterday, and she loved it. Last night, she called me, and we talked for like thirty minutes before her plane took off. My girl was probably at home sleeping right now, but it was three in the afternoon, so I was about to pop up on her and bring her some food.

"Hello, Ms. Cook, is Azia up yet?"

"Yes, I think she's getting out of the shower. You can wait in the living room."

"Okay. I brought us something to eat."

"Including me?" She laughed.

"Yes, including you."

Ms. Cook was so silly and down to earth. She will tell you how it is in a minute, though. She didn't hold her tongue for anyone.

Azia came down the stairs with her phone in her hand. She was cheesing hard, so she had to have been talking to D'Metrius. I had brought us some chicken wings, mac and cheese, string beans and potatoes, and rolls.

"Let's go get our nails and toes done," I suggested.

"Yes, I could use that. Let me change and grab my purse."

"Cool. I'm about to go to the car."

Azia came out about five minutes later, and I pulled off.

She hooked her phone up to the Bluetooth, and we jammed all the way to the nail place. It was a Tuesday, so it wasn't that crowded. Plus, my cousin worked there.

"Hey, Meila and Azia," my cousin greeted us when we walked in.

"Heeyy, boo," we both said. "Can you do our nails?"

"Yes, and my friend Kayla can do yours, Azia. She's really good unless you want to wait."

"No, that's fine, but I wanted my toes done too."

"Not a problem. Follow me, and I'll get you settled."

"Okay."

We followed her to the back of the shop, where they had the pedicure section decked the hell out. This was a woman's dream in a nail shop. They had a wine section with fruit and four types of wine. We sat in the massage chairs and sipped our drinks while watching TV.

"Girl, I got a date with D'Metrius tonight. I can't wait to get some of that dick."

"Ouuu, how you make that happen?"

I heard two girls talking a couple chairs down from me, and my eyes popped out of my head when I heard that shit. The girl said she saw him at the club last night, and they started talking. He asked her on a date, and she said yeah. I was gon' tell Azia, but I hoped it wasn't her D'Metrius because we were both gon' whoop his ass. The chick said they were going to this steakhouse on the north side.

I was about to tell Azia to call D'Metrius and see if she could see him tonight. If he came up with any excuses, then

I'd know what was up and tell her what I heard. We sat at the nail shop for another hour, and then we went back to Azia's house.

"You talked to D'Metrius today?" I asked.

"Yeah, earlier. He said he had some moves to make tonight, and we could hook up tomorrow. I probably will have to work, though. My boss said he'll let me know in another hour."

"Let's go get some steaks then. I know this great place on the north side, and we should go," I suggested. I wanted to see for myself; plus, I didn't want to be the bearer of bad news.

Azia agreed and said she'd meet me at my house at seven. I didn't know what time they would be there, but seven was cool with me. I drove home, praying that this nigga wouldn't do that to her. My girl would be so hurt because I believed she was really starting to like him.

Meka

"You feel like making breakfast, or you want me to drive?" Lucus asked me.

"I can cook breakfast. That's not a problem," I said and got up to turn the shower on.

Lucus had been at my place for the past three days, and I really enjoyed his company. He had been so sweet. Every day, he'd go to work and come back to me. He wasn't a nagger, and the dick was bomb. I could get used to this, but I wasn't ready to live with a man yet. I needed to get to know myself again before I could jump into a relationship. When he brought up the conversation yesterday, I told him I would think about it.

"Can I get in the shower with you?" Lucus asked.

"Yes, you can."

As soon as we got in the shower, he started kissing my

neck. Lucus moved his hands down my stomach and played with my clit, then he turned me around and stuck his dick in. As he pounded me from the back, he grabbed my hair and started playing with my clit again. I came twice, then he finally came.

"Best quickie I ever had," I said and smiled as I grabbed my rag to wash up.

"This dick right here is the best dick you'll ever have in your life." He smiled and grabbed his rag too.

"Oh, you're too cocky, huh?"

"Very."

We laughed and got out of the shower.

Lucus put on his sweatpants, and I put on some leggings and a t-shirt. We went downstairs, and since he was off today, I decided to cook breakfast and see how things were when we're together all day. Usually, he'd be at work, and that's how we got along so well.

I went into the kitchen and pulled out the waffle mix, hash browns, sausage, bacon, and eggs.

"Breakfast is served." I walked into the dining room and set our plates down.

"Damn, baby, this shit smells good as fuck."

"Just wait until you taste it."

He ate that food in one bite. I cleaned the table off and put the dishes in the dishwasher, then I went into the living room to watch a movie. My phone rang, and it was this nigga Ty. I didn't answer; I just let it ring. He kept calling, and now Lucus was looking at me funny because I wasn't answering my phone.

Knock! Knock! Knock!

I hope this nigga is not at my door, I thought as I huffed and puffed before getting up to get the door. When I peeked out the peephole, sure enough, this nigga was standing outside. I just didn't understand. I told this nigga two weeks ago that I was officially done, and we needed to lose contact. Now, there he was, right on my porch, knocking on my damn door.

"Ty, why are you here? If I didn't answer my phone the first three times, that doesn't mean show up at my house."

"Damn, why do you have to be so angry, baby? I was just stopping by because I was in the area."

"I'm not angry. I told you over and over again that we were done. Get off my porch, and make sure you take care of that newborn baby you just had," I snapped.

"Oh, you're mad because somebody else had my kid?"

"Nigga, trust me when I say I don't give two fucks. One less nigga I got to deal with. Now, get off my porch before I shoot yo' ass."

I had my gun in a little space by my door for easy grabs.

Slap!

That nigga slapped me, and when I looked back up, Lucus was on top of him.

"She just asked you to leave three times, three different ways, and I just beat yo' ass. Get the fuck on before you won't be able to walk."

Lucus turned me around, and we walked into the house. My face was red and swollen on the right side, so I grabbed an ice pack. I was heated, but I was glad I didn't have to shoot his ass. Now, hopefully, he got the fucking picture and would leave me the hell alone. I didn't want to get anyone else involved, but I wouldn't hesitate to tell my brother what was up. He should've kept his dick in his pants, but he didn't, and now he was miserable. He thought I cared because he had a damn baby... silly rabbit.

"Are you good?" Lucus asked.

"Yes, I'm fine. Thanks for helping me. I didn't want you involved. That's why I wasn't answering the phone for him."

"It's cool, that's what I'm here for, but the next time he comes over here, I'm killing his ass."

"I'll be right by your side," I assured him.

"Let's go get dressed. I got something I want to show you."

We went upstairs to get dressed. My blood boiled as I looked in the mirror at my face. It wasn't bad, but that shit was red. I had something for that nigga; this shit was not over at all. Ty didn't know who he was fucking with. I had some shit up my sleeve, and nobody was going to know what I was up to. We had put trackers on our phones, so we could always know where each other were. I thought it was harmless until one day, he showed up at my brother's house. He was upset because I wasn't answering the phone, but I didn't hear it, and he showed his ass.

Metri fought the nigga, and I had to save his ass that

time. That night, I snuck in his phone and erased the app. I told him that the app was a problem, and I couldn't have him popping up on me every time I didn't answer the phone. I never deleted my app, but I told him I did. I never popped up on him, but this time would be very different.

Wayne

"Aye, bro, you sure Hershey is the right way to get to her pops?" I asked D.

I had some information on a nigga who was trying to take over the city. We couldn't have that shit going on, so I had to let my nigga know. We came up with a plan, and I told him to try to get some information from her. He decided to take her to dinner and see what he could do. I knew where their trap house was because I had done some research of my own before I brought it to his attention.

"I don't know, but I'm gon' try to get some information and go from there."

"Well, be careful, bro. Me, Mike, Trey, and Lucus gon' go over to the trap house."

"How that nigga Lucus working out?"

"Shid, he's straight, bro. He doesn't do drama and will buss at a nigga quick."

"That's what I'm talking about. Alright, let me get to this business. I'll get up with you soon."

"Bet."

I hopped in the car and made some calls to the team. I told them to meet me at seven and bring their vests. The nigga Reggie was holding down the north side, and now the nigga wanted to expand and thought he was about to come into our territory. He had things fucked up. When I pulled up to my house, Rosalina, my baby mama, was sitting in her car. She was a damn headache. I wished I could take my son, and she could get the fuck on.

She was always on my case about something, and she always needed money. I told her she better find a nigga because that wasn't my job anymore. She cheated with a nigga who she told me was her friend from elementary, but all along, they were fucking. I put her ass out, then she came calling me two weeks later, talking about she was pregnant. I made sure I took a blood test, though.

"Rosalina, why are you here?"

"JR keeps calling your name, and you weren't answering the phone, so I came over."

"Where the hell is JR then if you brought him to see me?"

"I had to make sure you were here. I'll be right back."

"Yo, where the fuck you going? I can come get my son tonight when I'm done with this business."

"Whatever, Wayne. You're always on bullshit, and we don't need you."

"I'll get my son around nine, so have him packed and ready."

I went into the house and left her outside. She wanted me to say she could come in since she didn't have JR, but that situation was dead. I was starting to really like Kameila, and I knew she was feeling me, but I hadn't told her that I have a two-year-old son. I didn't know if she'd accept him, but I hoped she would.

Kameila was coming over tonight. This was not how I planned to tell her about my son, but I believed it was the right time.

By the time I had changed clothes, the crew had pulled up to my house. I locked my door and walked to the curb.

"Y'all niggas ready? It's time to head out."

"You know we stay ready."

"Bet."

We hopped in Lucus's truck and pulled off. The trap house was thirty minutes away, and I wanted to be parked and watching. There were three cars parked in front of the house and two people standing outside. We had parked across the street but a couple houses down, so we could have a clear view. Before we got out of the truck, two more people walked out of the house.

"Y'all ready?"

"Stay ready."

"Let's go."

We crept across the street with our masks on and our guns drawn. I saw one nigga trying to get in his car, and I shot his ass with my silencer; I didn't need any distractions. We were about to send a message to the plug not to fuck with the south side.

"Aye, nigga, when we get the south side on lock, we gon' be good."

I had walked up to a conversation, so I stood still.

"Yeah, but we got to get rid of them niggas."

"That shouldn't be a problem, right?" He pulled out his gun and started laughing.

"Not if we get to you first," I said as I stepped out of the shadows.

"Nigga, who the fuck?"

Before he could finish his sentence, I walked up and busted that nigga in his shit with my pistol.

Soon as I did, I had to duck because the other nigga started shooting. I called over the walkie-talkie and told my niggas to catch his ass. Somebody said he jumped in a car and left. Once I caught up with them, we set that trap house on fire. I had called D, but he didn't answer, so I texted him and told him to call me as soon as possible.

"Y'all niggas straight?"

"Yeah, we're good, except Luc got shot in the leg."

"I'll take you to the hood doctor, and he'll stitch you up, bro. You'll be good."

"I'm not tripping over this, but that's cool. My girl gon' be tripping, and I don't know how I'm gon' tell her this happened."

"She doesn't know what you're into, huh?"

"Hell nah, and I was trying to keep it from her ass," he said and laughed.

"That's a tough one, bro, because this game can go all kinds of ways. I suggest you tell her the truth and take it from there."

"Yeah, bro, I will."

I took Lucus to the hood doctor after we dropped them niggas off. The bullet went straight through, so he gave him some meds, and we left. Luc dropped me off at home and said he was good to drive to his girl's house.

Those south side niggas were about to be a big problem that we did not need. We stayed ready for the bullshit, though, so I wasn't worried about that shit. I just had to figure out some names and where those niggas be at because that trap house was gone.

Azia

"Are you ready to go get some steaks?" Kameila asked.

"Yes, I am. I'm hungry as hell."

"Let's go eat then, sis."

When we arrived at Ruth's Chris steakhouse, it was packed like they were selling drugs. We got out of the car looking cute as hell in our dresses and heels. Walking up to the door, I thought I saw D'Metrius' truck, but I didn't pay it any mind. I figured if they made one, they made another.

"Girl, it smells so damn good in here."

"I know. My stomach started gurgling as soon as we walked in."

"Hello, welcome to Ruth's Chris. May I have the name on your reservation?"

Kameila gave the hostess her name, and we were seated.

"Here are your menus. Staci will be your server, and she'll be over in just a second."

The server walked over to our table right after the hostess left.

"Hello, I'm Staci. Can I start you ladies off with anything to drink?"

"Yes, I'll have some lemon water for now," I said.

"I'll have some wine. Chardonnay will be fine," Kameila added, and I laughed. That girl loved some wine.

"Okay, I'll be right back."

When she left, we looked at the menu, and I wanted almost everything I saw. I decided to order a blue cheese crusted ribeye with a shrimp skewer, a loaded baked potato, and asparagus. Kameila ordered the prime rib au jus with mashed potatoes and corn. While I was sipping my water, I heard this lady laugh, and I just happened to look up. Guess who I saw?

"Girl, is that D'Metrius over there on a date?" Kameila said before I could question it myself.

"I was just about to say that. I'm about to call his phone and see what he says."

We were at a table in the back, and I could see him, but I could only see the back of the chick's head. He couldn't see me. I called his phone, and he didn't answer. When I called a second time, he got up to go to another area. I couldn't believe this nigga was on a date. That's why he had been so distant today. I called him earlier, and he said he'd be handling business today, and he could see me later.

"What's up, beautiful?"

"Hey, handsome. What are you doing?"

"Nothing much, just chilling, waiting on this phone call. What are you doing?"

"Oh, nothing, just downtown getting some steaks."

"Oh, for real? Where?"

"Ruth's Chris Steakhouse. It's kind of funny because I thought I saw you here."

"Nah, not me. I'll get up with you soon. My call just came through."

"Okay."

Although I acted as if everything was cool, I was boiling inside. I knew how to get back at his ass, though. I had to work tomorrow, so I was trying to chill with everyone before I left. For my next flight, I'd be gone for three days to Jamaica. I couldn't wait to feel some sun and have a drink or two. I just wished Kameila could come with me.

"What did he say, girl?" Kameila asked as soon as I hung up.

"Here's your order, ladies. Enjoy, and let me know if you need anything else," the server said as she placed our dishes on the table.

"Thank you," I said. Once she walked away, I looked at Kameila. "He said he's chilling, and he isn't at a steakhouse."

"Well, are we about to walk over there or nah?"

"Yup, let's go."

Walking over to the table, all I could think about was why he would lie like that. The table wasn't far from us, and when we got there, D'Metrius' eyes bucked. He looked shocked, and I knew I had caught his ass up with this one.

"So, this must be you at home chilling, huh?"

"I... I was just...."

"You were just what? Lying, nigga. You got me fucked up out here. Leading me on, making up lies and shit as you go, huh?"

"Hold up. Who the fuck is this? And why is she checking you?" his date piped up.

"Bitch, shut the fuck up unless you want these hands across your fucking face," I said.

"Bitch, who the fuck you calling a bit—"

Before she could finish, I slapped the shit out of her and pulled the bitch out of the booth. People ran over and tried to stop me. I was already mad, so no one could get me under control. That's why Kameila didn't try. D'Metrius tried and caught a punch to the side of his face. Security finally came over and put us out. We didn't even get to pay the bill but fuck them and this restaurant. I was sick of muthafuckas trying to play with me.

"You gon' be good, girl?" Kameila asked once we got to our cars.

"Yeah, I'll be straight. I'm about to get in the shower and get ready for work tomorrow."

"Call me if you need to talk, Azia."

"I will. Thank you for having my back."

"You already know I got you. I have to tell you something, though. Today at the nail shop, I heard that girl having a conversation with her friend. She said she was going on a date with D'Metrius. I didn't want to tell you. I wanted you to see it for yourself."

"So, you knew all this time that he'd be there and didn't even warn me?"

"Look, Azia, I didn't want to tell you false information, so I figured we'd just go and find out together."

"Oh, okay, so I guess it's make Azia look crazy day. Thanks, best friend."

I hopped in my car and blasted the music all the way home, thinking about what the fuck had just happened. D'Metrius had called me at least five times, but it was fuck him at this point, and he was going on the block list.

When I walked into the house, my mom was sitting on the couch, watching *Law and Order*. She loved that show. She watched the reruns all day long on her off days.

"Hey, baby, how was your day?"

"It was exhausting."

"What happened? Tell Mama all about it."

That's what I did. I told my mother everything, and she told me I was wrong for treating Kameila that way. It wasn't her fault, and she just wanted me to see it for myself. I got that, but she could've at least warned me. Still, I called her and apologized for having an attitude, and she apologized for not telling upfront. I loved Kameila like a sister, and she only wanted the best for me like I did for her.

I went upstairs, turned the shower on, and wrapped my hair. My damn feet were hurting from those heels, and I had the nerve to be fighting. I was so over today, and I was happy to pull out my Kindle and read a book until I fell asleep.

D'Metrius

a whole week had passed since I'd last talked to Azia, and I was pissed that she didn't even let me explain. When she walked up to the table, I was so shocked that I started stuttering and shit; I couldn't believe myself. I called her phone, but I guess she had me blocked. I even went to her house, and her mom said she wasn't home. At that point, I didn't know what to do, but I had some business to handle.

We had to go back to Miami because Dhillon wanted to have a meeting tomorrow. I was on my way to pick up Punch and head to the airport. We hadn't heard shit from them southside niggas, but I knew some shit was gon' pop off, and I would be ready when they tried to retaliate. Niggas weren't gon' take that shit lying down, especially fucking with their money.

I pulled up to Punch's house and called to let him know I was outside.

"Aye, bro, you ready?"

"Yeah, I'm walking out now, bro."

"You heard anything else about them niggas?" I asked once he got in the car.

"I was just about to tell you one of them niggas shot Ty last night. He in the hospital now. We don't know what the outcome is yet."

"Man, fuck. I knew burning up that house was gon' be a fucking problem."

"Take that shit up with Lucus. He had the gasoline and was mad 'cause they shot his ass."

"Niggas got to be more careful and think shit out."

"Yeah, I know, bro."

When we got to the airport, I found a spot in the lot near the terminal and parked my car. We didn't bring any bags because I was sure we were going to drive back. I didn't know what the meeting was about; he just said to come see him in the morning. We had to rush again because we were late as hell, and the plane was literally about to start boarding. Dhillon said a car would be at the airport when we get off the plane.

It didn't take us long to get on or off the plane, and when we walked outside the airport in Miami, there was an all-black Tahoe waiting for us.

"What's up, man?" I greeted the driver.

The nigga standing by the door didn't even say shit.

"Damn, is he deaf or something?" Punch said.

"I don't know. Nigga, this my first time seeing him. Remember, it was another nigga here last time."

"Yeah, you're right, but I got this feeling, bro, that isn't sitting well with me."

"Everything gon' be good, bro. It's just a meeting. I did call my uncle and ask him if he would be at the meeting, but he said he didn't know shit about it."

"See, that's that bullshit right there. You know my instincts are always right, bro," Punch said.

I sat there for a minute then decided to text my uncle. He said he hadn't heard anything, but he was still coming since I mentioned it. I wondered why Dhillon would tell me and Punch to come but not my uncle. We were all on the same team, so that wasn't sitting well with me. When we pulled up to the house, there were about three cars parked in the wraparound driveway.

"What's up, guys? You might hurry up and take a seat," Dhillon said when we walked in.

"Why, what's the rush?" Punch asked.

"I'm ready to get this over with. I have a hot date tonight."

"Yeah, okay."

We grabbed a chair and sat down to discuss business. It was the same ole bullshit to me and shit we should already know. I wasn't feeling all those old ass dudes staring and shit, so I went to the bathroom to text my uncle and see where he was. I couldn't find any damn signal in that big ass house; I even walked to the back of the kitchen, and still no signal.

"Bro, there's something else going on in here. I just heard some screaming in the basement. I went to the back of the kitchen to try to get a signal, and I can't get that either," I whispered to Punch after I walked back into the living room and took my seat.

Before he could respond, Dhillon interrupted us. "Do you guys not know how to pay attention?"

"We are paying attention. What are you talking about?" I challenged.

"You have been having a conversation since both of you got here. Now, this is business, and I have one more thing left to say. That trap house that your crew burned down on the south side was also my shit, and I don't appreciate the way you went about things."

"Well, I wasn't having nobody trying to take over my territory. Them niggas should've stayed where they were."

"I figured you'd be a smart ass, just like your fucking uncle."

"Speaking of him, why wasn't he at the meeting?"

"Because this wasn't his meeting. Any more issues you want to discuss?"

"Nah, I'll just take the work, so we can get back home."

Punch and I followed Dhillon to his office, and he sat in the chair while looking under his desk. I heard those screams again and looked at Punch. He was already looking at me.

Dhillon grabbed a book from under his desk and set it in front of us. He had my uncle's name written in there like twenty times for being late on a payment, getting robbed, etc. He kept a book of everything, but I didn't know what he was showing me for. My name wasn't in that book.

"Why are you showing us this?" I asked.

"Because your name and his name are going in this spot right here. Why, you ask? Because your crew blew up a trap house with fifty thousand dollars' worth of my product in there. I want my money, or your little girlfriend who works at the airport, you won't see her again."

"Don't fuck with her. She doesn't have shit to do with this. Furthermore, I'm not paying you shit because you should've told your little soldiers to stay put on their side. That's your fault, not ours!"

"I told you something was up with this meeting, bro," Punch muttered.

"Should've followed your friend's advice."

"You could've told me this shit through a phone call."

Dhillon got up to leave, so I guess we were dismissed. I could already tell this nigga was about to be a whole problem. Fucking with Azia, that shit is off-limits. So I had to come up with a plan to take this nigga out. As we were walking out, one of his men was standing in the foyer. I could see his phone, and he was watching someone getting beat. It seemed to be a camera connected to his phone, and that shit was in the basement. That was the screaming and shit I had heard this whole time. Dhillon and his crew were weird. He had to go if he thought he was about to do anything to the people I cared about.

"Bro, if he knows where Azia works, I'm quite sure he knows about Meka and Kameila."

"Yeah, bro, we have to get back home. Let's go get in this truck."

Everyone was gone except the dude who had brought us there.

We got to the airport and boarded our flight back to Chicago. I prayed that Azia was home and she would talk to me. She needed to know what was going on, and I had to tell her what she didn't want to hear—that I sold drugs. She had asked me twice, and I just told her no. I told her my mom had an insurance policy, and Meka and I got ten thousand each.

Azia

For the past week, I had felt like someone was watching me. I called Kameila and told her, but she said I was being paranoid. Today, I had to go to the grocery store and get some food for the week. It was a good day; I hadn't been called to work in two days, and I was happy as shit because I needed some rest and relaxation. I wanted some fried lobster tails, loaded potatoes, and broccoli. My mom was off work, and I was going to cook dinner for us. I wanted to tell her that I had found a house, and I was moving on Monday. It was last minute, but I couldn't pass up the opportunity to get my first home.

"Good morning, Mom. I'm about to go to the market. I'll be right back."

"Okay, hurry back. I found a good movie to watch."

Trying to decide if I wanted to go to Walmart or the grocery store, I figured I'd just go around the corner to the grocery store. Walmart was like twenty minutes away compared to the grocery store's five minutes. After pulling into my spot close to the door, I looked around the parking lot. Nothing seemed out of place, so I grabbed my purse and went in.

"Hey, girl, what are you up to this early?" Kameila had FaceTimed me.

"Nothing, girl, just doing a little food shopping since me and Mama are both off. What are you doing?"

"Ouuu, sounds like you're cooking breakfast or brunch. I want some. I'm just lying here, watching LMN."

"That's your favorite network, and you know you can have some. You don't live across the street anymore, so you better get dressed."

"Yeah, I know. I'll call you when I'm on my way."

"Okay."

I had to grab some butter, eggs, and pancake mix, but I ended up getting some of everything I didn't need. The grocery store wasn't crowded, so that was a great thing. While turning the corner toward the dairy section, I saw this guy make the same turn as me. Now, I knew this was a grocery store, but this man looked creepy, and I was about to get in line.

"Excuse me, miss."

I turned around. "Yes?" I wasn't going to be rude since I had nothing to protect me.

"You're D'Metrius' girlfriend, right?"

"I'm a friend of his."

"Tell him an old friend is looking for him," he said and walked out the door.

I watched as he jumped in that same truck that I saw following me a couple of days ago. *So, does that mean he knows where I live?* This couldn't be happening. What the fuck was D'Metrius into that had people looking for him?

I hurriedly paid for my things, then went home. I was about to call him as soon as I put these bags down.

"Why are you looking at me like that?" I asked my mom. She was acting strange.

"No reason. You have company in the kitchen, sweetie."

"Kameila didn't even call and say she was on her way."

I walked into the kitchen, about to cuss Kameila out, but it wasn't her. Shocked was an understatement for how I felt, and my heart was beating faster than it was at the grocery store. I hadn't seen this dude in almost two weeks, and he was looking like an entire all-you-can-eat buffet. I wanted to kiss those lips and take his ass to my room. We hadn't had sex yet, but damn he was tempting.

"D'Metrius, what are you doing here?"

"We have to talk. I've been calling you for damn near two weeks, Azia."

"I know, D'Metrius, but your little date fucked that up."

"I wasn't out on a date. Look, can we talk somewhere more private?"

"Yes."

I took him up the stairs to my bedroom. There were boxes everywhere because I was packing. D'Metrius looked around and sat on the bed after moving some things. I sat in the chair at my desk and looked at him, waiting for him to start the conversation.

"Listen, I know you don't want to hear this, but you have to. I have been selling drugs with Punch, and now we have some people coming after us and our loved ones. We had an incident the night I saw you at the steakhouse."

"Wait, so you're telling me that ten-thousand-dollar insurance policy was a lie?"

"No, that's true, but I didn't tell you what I did for a living because you have said plenty of times that you weren't dealing with drug dealers. I couldn't tell you this because I like you a whole lot, Azia. I'm not trying to do this drug shit all my life. It's a long story, but I need you to be careful. You know how to shoot a gun?"

"Uh, no. I don't do guns either. Who's coming after you, or me, or all of us?"

"Listen, Dhillon, my connect, is trying to say I owe him fifty thousand dollars because my crew burnt up his trap house. I didn't know that was his trap house until we went to the meeting yesterday. He said he knows where you work, and he could get you any time. So, I had to come warn you and let you know that I'll always be around because I refuse to let anyone touch you."

"I appreciate that, but I'm moving. I found a house that's ten minutes away from the airport. While we're on the subject, this guy walked into the grocery store this morning and said to tell you an old friend is looking for you. Now, what's this issue about?"

"I don't know, Azia, for real, but I'll figure it out. Sounds like the same nigga who walked up to Meka at her house."

"He was dark-skinned and tall. He got in a red truck."

"Thanks for that information. I promise I'll figure this out. Where do we go from here, though?"

"Honestly, I don't know. I'm really starting to like you. What was that date about?"

"It wasn't a date, Azia. It was a business plan. Yes, I knew she liked me, but I wasn't on that type of time. I needed her out the way. She's Dhillon's daughter. Her name is Hershey, and he doesn't know that I know her. He thinks she's safe, but I got something for them both."

I sat in the chair and just thought about this news. D'Metrius had really dropped a couple bombs on me in one sentence, but I couldn't let this man out of my life because of a few obstacles. I didn't know what he had over me, and we hadn't even had sex. This was a new one for me, but I liked it, and I liked the feeling I got when I was around him.

"I understand everything you're saying, and I'll be by your side."

"Are you serious right now, Azia?" He was smiling so hard.

"Yes, I'm serious. You can teach me how to shoot on my off days, and we'll go from there."

D'Metrius grabbed me up and started kissing me like he hadn't seen me in years. I began to get butterflies again.

Once he started rubbing on me, I was ready to drop my clothes. Unfortunately, my mom was downstairs, and that couldn't happen, so I stopped him. I needed to cook my food and let my mom know what was going on.

"Can you help me move my things into my house tonight?"

"I'll do anything you need me to."

"Aren't you sweet? You can come back at six if you're not busy."

"Alright, I'll be here."

D'Metrius kissed me again, and then he went downstairs to leave. I sat on the bed and just reminisced about his kisses. The two boyfriends I had before D'Metrius were nothing like him, maybe because they didn't sell drugs. Kilwin was a computer freak; he could break into anything. He took me to a robot competition once, and I enjoyed myself, but it wasn't my cup of tea. Luckily, he went off to college in Mississippi. Symon was just a straight asshole at times. He had a temper and used to just pop up everywhere. I had to leave his ass alone and let him get his shit in order.

I went downstairs and started the food. My mom was asleep on the couch, and Kameila had called and said she'd be over shortly.

Meka

"Why are you looking at me like that, Lucus?" I asked.

"Because you're hungry, and you won't tell me what you want to eat."

"I don't know. I just said that a million times already."

I still had an attitude with him because he had been lying to me about his occupation all this time. This nigga worked for my brother. I found that out the night he got shot. He came hopping in the house at about eleven at night and thought I would've been upstairs. I wasn't mad at the fact that he was a drug dealer, but it was the fact that he had been lying all this time.

"Listen, I know you're mad because of the lie I told, but I apologized over and over again, baby."

"Does Metri know that we're together?"

"Nobody knows who I talk to. I don't like to talk about my business."

"Cool, let's keep it that way for a while."

"Are we good now? Because I can't take you being mad at me."

"Yes, we're good."

"Can you tell me what we're eating, please?"

"I still don't know. Get some fish and chicken."

"Bet. I'm going to take a quick shower, then I'll go to the store," Lucus said and headed upstairs.

I was off work today, and I just wanted to relax. Since I had the insurance money that my mom left me, it was time to think about what I wanted to do with my future. I had been thinking about opening my own boutique to sell women's and little girl's clothing. I had an eye for fashion, and it was time to stop playing and do what I wanted.

My phone rang and seeing my brother's face pop up on the screen, I immediately answered.

"Meka, I'm on my way over there. I need to talk to you," Metri said.

"Okay."

I guess he was going to find out about Lucus and me today. I wasn't worried and him knowing; it's just that I knew the big brother instinct would kick in, and then he'd be all in my business. Metri sounded like he really needed to talk, and I was curious to know what this was about. Since our mother died, he hadn't been around that much. He'd been trying to keep himself busy. I didn't blame him because I was doing the same thing. I was using Lucus as a distraction, but my feelings for him had grown.

"What's up, bro?" I said when I opened the door for Metri.

"Is that Lucus' car outside?"

"Yes, it is. What did you want to talk about?"

"How the... Look, never mind. Dhillon, my connect, is on some bullshit. I need you to be careful and have your gun on you at all times."

"What the hell? Is he after Lucus too?"

"He's probably going to come after all of us because I'm not paying him fifty thousand dollars."

"How the hell do you owe that much money to the connect, Metri?"

"Listen, he got some new people on his team. He put them on the south side and tried to take over here. We had to send them a message, and someone thought it might be a good idea to burn the house down."

"Well, whoever idea it was should be the one paying his ass."

"That would be your little boyfriend because he got shot."

Lucus came downstairs just in time. He didn't know Metri was there. To find out all this bullshit, and he was the cause of it all, I couldn't believe what I was hearing. That's why I wanted my brother to go legit. The drug game was death waiting to happen. People took that shit seriously, especially when someone was fucking with their money.

"Your bright idea was to blow up the house with the drugs inside. Now Dhillon wants fifty thousand dollars, or he's coming after everybody," Metri told Lucus.

"Man, fuck that nigga. I'm not scared of no nigga who bleeds just like me."

"With that mindset, you're going to get fucked up too," I said.

"Nigga, this isn't about if you're scared. This nigga is trying to come for my family, and I'm not having that. Either get your mind right, or you can get the fuck on," Metri said and walked out the door.

I was in disbelief; this fool was really tripping. He was gon' have to get the hell on at this point. Lucus didn't tell me all this shit when he told me he got shot. See, this was why I needed to just focus on myself and try to start this boutique. I wanted to move somewhere else, but I didn't know where yet.

Shaking my head at the foolishness, I went into the kitchen and started cooking some fish and shrimp with French fries since Lucus didn't get a chance to go to the store. By the time I was done cooking, I had lost my appetite, so I decided to head to the mall. I needed some retail therapy. That always kept my mind off the negative things that were going on. I needed to go back to school, so I could get my business started, and I definitely needed to find a house. If that other dude could find me, then this damn Dhillon fool could too. This shit was stressing me out.

"I'll be back. If you leave, lock the door and put the key

under the light outside," I told Lucus before I went outside and got in my car.

When I got to the mall, I pulled into a parking spot and made sure my gun was in my purse. As I walked through the mall, I went into almost every store. I had about five bags already. They had a smoothie station in the food court, and I wanted a strawberry banana. A text came through on my phone as I waited in line to order my smoothie.

Lucus: I'm going to check on my mother. I'll be back tomorrow.

Me: Okay, cool.

Lucus: That's all you have to say?

Me: Yes, I'll see you tomorrow.

Once I finished at the mall, I decided to get my nails and toes done. My best friend had gone back out of town for school. Key was in law school at Columbia University in New York. She graduated from the University of Chicago last year, and I was so proud of her. My girl made it out the hood at only twenty-two—most people didn't even make it that long.

I was digging in my purse and not paying attention as I walked to the car when a hand came across my mouth. I couldn't scream or anything because whatever was on the cloth had knocked me out.

Kameila

I had been up all night and this morning baking these damn edibles. Finally, I was finished, and now I had to start getting ready for the party. I was with Wayne last night at his house, where I found out he has a two-year-old son. He was such a sweet kid and looked exactly like his father. I was cool with Wayne having a kid; that didn't matter. As long as the baby mother kept her space, we'd be cool. I called Azia to see if she wanted to go with me, and she agreed. She was going to meet me at my house and follow me to the party. She said she had something to tell me, and it sounded pretty serious. Wayne had told me about Dhillon and how I should watch my back. I couldn't believe those niggas were that reckless.

"Hey, sis, I'm here." I heard Azia walk through the door.

"Hey, I'm in the back."

"Ouu, this room is big. I can't believe this is my first time seeing your house."

"You're always at work or sleeping. Plus, you don't like to drive."

"You know driving irritates my soul, but I have some great news. I moved ten minutes from here."

"Whaattt, are you serious? Oh my god, that is so good, Azia."

"Yes, it was time for me to get my own space."

"Agreed."

We both laughed, and I finished getting ready before we packed the car and left. Damon had texted me the address already, and I was like five minutes late. Luckily, I was a fast driver and could make a long drive into a short one. I grabbed my purse and boxes, and we left the house. I had been looking into the information I needed to start my dispensary. I'd also been looking for a job because the money I had saved was almost gone.

"You finally made it! You can set your things up here," Damon said when we arrived.

"I apologize for being late," I told him.

"You know I don't trip. Now, if you didn't show up, then we'd have a problem." Damon gave me a hug, and I introduced him to Azia.

"Now, you know when it's money to be made, I'll be in the building, I said," and we all laughed.

We set up the table and the *Mei and My Buds* banner. It was a name that Azia and I had come up with a couple months ago when I brought up the idea of opening a business.

"Hey, is your name Ka-mei-la?"

"It is. May I help you with something?"

"I think you know my baby daddy, Wayne, and I'm gon' need you to leave him alone."

"Did you even hear what you just said? Your *baby daddy*, not boyfriend or husband. So, if you can go back over there and mind your business, I'd greatly appreciate it."

"You heard what I said."

That bitch was crazy if she thought she could scare me away from Wayne. I put that shit in the back of my mind and continued to do my job. I had actually done well and made five hundred dollars in three hours. Azia was in the bathroom; she had eaten a brownie and was getting paranoid. I told her to put some water on her face.

"Bitch, those brownies got me seeing double," Azia said when she returned.

"Yo' ass don't smoke weed and have never tried to. I don't even know why you ate that here."

"Shit, they bought up everything. I had to at least try it," she said, and we laughed.

"You did a great job, Mei, and everybody is talking about those brownies and mac and cheese. I should've gotten me some, but I was busy hosting and shit," Damon walked up and said.

"Thank you, D. I'm really glad you invited me. This

party was fun, even though I stayed over here. I'll make you some and bring them to you later this week."

"That sounds great. I can't wait. Thank you for coming, and I'll talk to you later." He turned to Azia. "See you, Azia. It was nice meeting you."

"Same here!" she said.

We packed up the table and started loading the trunk. As soon as I closed the trunk, Wayne's raggedy-ass baby mama was standing there. Azia walked up beside me and tilted her head while looking at her.

"What the fuck you want now?" I asked.

"I know you were around my son the other day too. Better keep your fucking distance."

"Listen, any problems you have, take that shit up with Wayne. You making yourself look stupid out here yapping them dick suckers at me."

She slapped me, and all I saw was red. I punched her ass so hard she fell on the hood of her car. Then I dragged her off the car and started pounding her some more. Azia pulled me off the girl, and she ran up and pulled my hair. I fell on the ground, and she tried to get on top of me, but I kicked her ass in her stomach. She fell back, and Damon ran over to us with some other people to break up the fight. I was furious that she made me act that way at an event I had just worked.

"Why the hell are you fighting my cousin, Mei?" Damon asked.

"She's mad because I'm talking to her baby daddy. She started with me, D. She slapped me!"

"She gets on my nerves, always trying to fight over that nigga. I apologize for this."

We got in our cars, and on the drive home, my head started hurting. I didn't even know how that bitch knew who I was. I was going to call Wayne when I got home and let him know he needed to keep his dogs on a leash. Next time, she would catch a bullet, and that's on me. JR better get used to me because he'll be mommy less if she tried this dumb shit again.

As I pulled into the driveway, I saw Wayne's car. I got out, and before I could close my car door, he was right behind me.

"Listen, I know my baby mother can be a childish ass person. I apologize that this happened. She called me screaming about y'all fighting. And she said I can't see JR anymore if I'm still gonna be messing with you. It's the same song, just a different tune."

"All I want to know is how does she know me or my name?"

"She was over my house the other day, dropping off JR, and I was in the kitchen. You had texted my phone, and it was on the living room table. She read the text, and we got into it. She wants to be with me, but I don't want her. I want you, Kameila. Like, real talk, I've been missing you."

I stood there for a minute and looked at Wayne to see if he was serious. Then I smiled and walked up to him.

Wayne grabbed me and started kissing me. Once he finally let me go, I unlocked the door and went to start the shower. When I looked at my face in the mirror, it was red and a little swollen. She had put a little power in that slap, but I bet she won't try that shit again.

D'Metrius

I had been at Azia's new house for the past two days. She had moved some of her things that night and the rest yesterday. While I took a shower before I headed to meet up with Punch, she was downstairs putting things away. I had been trying to contact Meka all morning, but she hadn't been answering her phone. So, I was gon' do a pop up and make sure that nigga Lucus hadn't done anything to my sister.

"Good morning. How did you sleep?" Azia asked when I joined her in the living room.

"That bed is actually comfortable. I don't know why you ordered another one."

"It's a new house, and I just want new things. The living room furniture will be here later. Hopefully, they'll put it together for me."

"I can put it together. Just call me when it gets here."

"Where are you going? You didn't even eat breakfast."

"I have a few moves to make, and I need to check on Meka. She hasn't been answering her phone this morning."

"Oh, no. I'm sure everything is fine, though. Call me later."

Azia gave me a hug, and I kissed her soft lips. She then smiled and went back to the couch to finish unpacking boxes.

I walked to my truck and hooked up my Bluetooth. Something wasn't sitting right with me, so I called Lucus. He said he didn't stay there last night. He and Meka got into an argument, and he left earlier in the day. My next call was to Punch. I told him to meet me at Meka's house. We pulled up at the same time.

"What up, bro?" he said.

"I'm trying to figure out where Meka is. She's not answering her phone, and she's not in the house."

"You checked her cameras?"

"Not yet."

Looking at the cameras, nothing seemed out of the ordinary until I saw a red truck ride past. That had me thinking about what Azia said happened at the grocery store. That part about *an old friend looking for you* popped in my head. Now, who the fuck was an old friend who could be looking for me?

"Bro, a few weeks ago, Meka said this dude came up to her over here and told her an old friend is looking for me. Then, Azia told me the same thing happened to her at the grocery store, and he got into a red truck. That red truck in the video is the same one she described."

"Okay, do you remember getting into it with someone back in the old days?"

"Nah, bro, this shit is crazy, and I need to figure this out."

"Bro, we gon' figure this shit out together. I need you to get yo' head together and try to remember something. It has to be something that happened in the past, and it's coming back."

I sat on Meka's couch and texted Azia to see if she was cool. She was good and chilling before work in a couple of hours. Then I thought about that mission I had when I was like eighteen or nineteen years old. This dude named Malik was the king at breaking into people's houses.

I was down and out one day, and I needed some money. He was about to hit a lick and was looking for one more person. My friend at the time, Ryan, asked me to join them. I agreed, and everything was going smoothly until we got outside, and the owners were pulling into the driveway. The man jumped out of the car and started shooting at us. We ran, and I turned around to see where Ryan was, but he was lying on the ground. I walked back to him, and he looked at me before he passed out. Once I heard sirens, I knew the police were close, so I had to get the hell out of there.

"Let's go see Andrew. Maybe he can find this person for me," I said.

"What person, bro? What happened?" Punch asked.

"It's a long story, but this nigga I did a mission with like five years ago might be back for revenge. I thought he died on the sidewalk, and the police were close to the scene, so I had to go."

"Yeah, you gon' tell me about that shit later. Let's go."

I called Andrew, and he was at the spot, so we headed that way. I couldn't believe this shit was happening. My cell phone rang, and it was from a private number. I didn't answer private numbers, so I ignored it. Then the shit rang again, and it was the same thing. I picked it up this time.

"Who the fuck is this?"

"I guess you didn't get my message, huh?"

"Nigga, who the fuck are you?"

"Your old friend, muthafucka. The one you left lying on the concrete five years ago."

"Ryan, you got my fucking sister?"

"Oh, now you remember me? And yes, I do. She's doing fine for now."

"What the fuck do you want?"

"I want my cut from the shit we stole, and I want double for the time I had to do and didn't rat you lame ass niggas out. I got shot in the chest, and I could've died. As soon as I was better, they shipped my ass to prison."

"Listen, that doesn't have shit to do with my sister. How much are you asking for?"

"Fifty thousand dollars. I want it tonight, or your precious sister dies. I'll text you the address when it's time."

He hung up the phone, and I let out a huge sigh. This shit was unbelievable. I had to come up with a plan to get this fool because he was tripping. That was five years ago, and we only got like five hundred off the shit. Splitting that with four people wasn't shit. I moved a couple weeks after that, and I hadn't seen or heard from them again until today.

"This nigga said he wants fifty thousand tonight, or he's killing Meka," I said to Punch.

"We know that shit is not happening, bro. We have to get the team together."

"Bet. Call and tell them to meet us at the spot in one hour."

We made it to Andrew, and I asked him to look up Ryan Mullins. It showed that he lived in Atlanta, but he had a sister who still lived in Chicago. She lived on the west side. We were gon' ride and see what was up with her. It also showed that he only did three years in jail. He'd been out for two years, probably plotting his revenge. I didn't know why he was after me, though. Those other niggas were his family.

"He called me private, so you can't track the number, but let's go check out his sister before we have to go to the spot," I said.

I sped to Ryan's sister's house, weaving in and out of traffic. When I pulled up, the house was dark, and there were no cars in the driveway. Punch went up and knocked on the door while I walked to the back to see if I could find anything. All I found was an old, raggedy pickup truck with no wheels and a rusted playground set.

"Nobody is in this muthafucka. It's dark as hell, and I don't even see any movement." Punch said when I met him on the porch.

"Man, fuck. This some bullshit. Let's go in and see what we can find." This shit was pissing me off; I needed to find my damn sister.

"This shit is fucked up. It looks like she just got up and moved. Only packed the important shit."

"Hell, yeah. He probably warned her that I'll be coming for his ass. Look at this picture I just found on the floor."

"Say it ain't fucking so, bro."

"The proof is right here. This the bitch that I took to dinner for our little plan that night. So, that means Ryan is her brother, and Dhillon is his pops."

"He's trying to get down on us, bro. We got to get to Meka."

"We have to get to the spot and see what address he sends us."

When we pulled up to the spot, everyone's cars were outside. I didn't know what we were about to do, but we had two hours to come up with something. We walked into the building and stood in the middle of the floor. I explained to them what had happened and what needed to be done about it.

"Call Andrew and see if he can track Meka's phone. This nigga is playing games, and I don't have all day," I told Punch.

"Bet."

Meka

When I finally woke up, I was tied to a chair, and the house I was in smelled like mothballs. This dude walked up to me with a knife and dragged it across my face. I was terrified. I didn't know this man or where I was. It was cold as hell in this basement, and I couldn't stop shaking. There was a couch against the wall along with two chairs and a table.

"Who are you, and what do you want from me?"

"No need to exchange names. Just know that if your brother doesn't have my money in an hour, you won't see him again."

"You the guy who came to my house that day."

"I told you I'll be back, but you didn't listen."

"I was out shopping, minding my business. Why are you being a creep and following me?"

"You are kind of cute, but I needed to show your brother

that I'm not about games. I want the money that's owed to me or else."

"Why kidnap me, though? I don't have anything to do with that."

"You're his precious sister. I knew he'd come for you."

He pulled out a bottle of liquor and drank half of it in one gulp. This man looked disgusting. I remembered Metri telling me that Dhillon wanted fifty thousand from him. This man didn't look like a drug dealer, so it couldn't be him. I wished Metri would get the hell out of the game and go legit because I didn't want to end up dead. I didn't want to have to look over my shoulder every damn day either. Now I was stuck with this lunatic, and he was a drunk.

"Come on, it's time to go. You better hope your brother got my cash."

I didn't say anything; I just prayed that whatever Metri was up to worked.

The man untied me from the chair and quickly tied my arms behind my back. He put me in the backseat of this red truck and pulled off. Once we got on the road, he turned his music up so loud that the speakers in the door were rambling.

I started playing with the knot on the rope. While he drove, I kept trying to loosen my restraints. When I finally got myself untied, I was so happy. I sat there for a minute, trying to figure out my next move. I didn't know where he was taking me.

"We're almost there. You better start praying that your brother has my money."

"He got your money. Remember, I'm his precious sister."

Once he pulled into a driveway and I saw Metri's truck, I quietly unlocked the door and ran like a bat out of hell over to my brother's vehicle.

The guy was screaming and yelling, then all of a sudden, I heard gunshots. I didn't know where they were coming from. So, I jumped in the truck, and when I turned around, that dude was lying on the ground.

Metri and Punch jumped in the truck and pulled off.

"Listen, sis, I apologize for all of this. I didn't know that nigga was still alive. He came after me to get revenge for some shit that happened five years ago. Man, fuck, that's another body that we have to get rid of," Metri said.

"It's not your fault that he's a lunatic, bro. I understand fully about the consequences that come with this game. I do want you to go legit, though, because next time, I might not be so lucky. I'll help y'all get rid of his ass, though."

"You're not helping with nothing. We are about to drop you off and have our boys come handle this," Metri insisted.

"Okay, fine."

Metri dropped me off at his house, and they pulled off again. I went into the bathroom that he had downstairs and got in the shower. After putting on a pair of my brother's jogging pants and a t-shirt, I felt way better. I called Lucus, but he didn't answer the phone. Since I had some time on my hands, I started looking on the internet for houses. I needed a new place to stay and a new job.

Ciera from the bar called me about thirty minutes later. "Hey, girl, are you coming to work today?"

"No, girl, I got a lot going on right now. I'll be in tomorrow night."

"Well, I was just letting you know that Leon said if you don't show up tonight, you're fired."

"Girl, fuck him and that bar. All he thinks about is himself. I have been gone for three days. I don't even miss work, so if he's about to trip over this, he can get the fuck on."

"I feel you, girl. I'll let him know."

"Okay."

I couldn't believe Leon. I had texted him and told him that I would be off for three days before this shit even happened. Shit, I was tired of going to that bar anyway. It was always crowded with the same people, and I knew just about everyone who walked through the door. Men old enough to be my granddaddy had tried to talk to me. Furthermore, I got tired of coming home smelling like smoke.

Metri had told me to stay at his house, but I needed to go up to the mall and see if my car was still there. Before I could order an Uber, Lucus called me back.

"Baby, I apologize. I didn't hear my phone. I was helping... Well, you know what's up. How are you feeling?"

"I'm feeling better. I need to go see if my car is still at the mall."

"Text me the address where you are. I'm on my way."

"Okay."

I texted Lucus Metri's address, and I asked him to stop by my house and grab me some clothes. I couldn't walk around looking like a boy with my brother's clothes on. Metri called to check on me, and I told him I was good and that Lucus was on his way to get me. He told me to be careful, and he'd call me later.

Lucus pulled up a few minutes after Metri called. I was so glad to see him, and I melted into his arms as soon as I opened the door.

"I'm glad he didn't hurt you," Lucus said.

"Yeah, me too."

I locked up my brother's house and got in the car with Lucus. After a few minutes, he turned the radio down and looked over at me.

"I was thinking about us moving in together, buying our own house, and starting in a better place. I know I have some flaws, but we all do. I want you to be happy, and me being happy is with you."

"That doesn't sound bad. We're practically living together at my house. I'll give it a try. Being with you is my happy place also."

"Glad to hear that. Now I have this house I want you to look at."

"Okay. My car should be over here in the back by the stores."

I lost my purse, so I had to get a tow truck to tow it home. I was just happy it was still there. The tow truck took forty-five minutes to come, and I happily gave them the address where they needed to take it.

Azia

I loved my new house and all the new things I had put into it. My mom was so happy that I let her decorate the bathrooms and the kitchen. She was sad to see me go but proud of my accomplishments. No matter what, I would always be a mama's girl, so we would still see each other often.

This morning, I had to be at work by 10:00, and I didn't feel like going. I liked the job, though. It wasn't much to it. Those seats were very uncomfortable, but the paychecks were nice, and I didn't plan to stop any time soon.

"Good morning, baby," Metri said.

"Good morning."

"It's seven in the morning. Why do you have the shower on?"

"Babe, I told you last night, I'll be gone for two days. I have to go to work."

"I don't remember. I was too focused on tearing that sweet pussy up."

"Yeah, I had a really good time last night," I said and smiled.

"Let me get in the shower with you, and I can send you to work feeling even better."

"Let's go."

I ran to the bathroom and got in the shower. The water was so hot; it felt like a Jacuzzi. As soon as D'Metri got in, he grabbed me and turned me toward him. He kissed me so gently, and I quivered at his touch. This man was never rough with me. He rubbed my body so smoothly and started playing with my clit. I almost climbed up the shower wall.

"Don't be running. Take this dick, baby."

D'Metrius threw the shower curtain over the rail and sat on the edge of the tub. I got on top and started riding him like I was driving a sports car. I was going up and down and twerking my ass cheeks on the dick. When I turned around and grabbed his ankles, I made sure this ass was bouncing. We came at the same time, then grabbed our rags and started washing up.

"Damn, girl. That was the shit."

"Oh, really? I'm glad you liked it."

"Yeah, I can get used to this. It's us forever, baby. I'm gon' show you better than I can tell you."

"So, what does that mean?"

"Azia, do you want to be in a relationship with me?

We've been doing this dating thing for about four months now."

"Oouu, you're keeping count. I like that. But, yes, I would love to be your woman."

"You had me nervous for a minute."

"You weren't nervous, fool. You already knew my answer."

After our shower, I went downstairs to make us something quick to eat. Since I still had two hours before I needed to leave, I was about to chill with my new man. I made breakfast that consisted of sausage, bacon, eggs, grits, and biscuits with orange juice to wash it down. D'Metrius didn't know I could cook the way I had done for the past four days that he'd been with me. I hadn't even gone anywhere. I had been in this house, watching TV, reading books, and cooking.

"It's time for me to leave, baby. I'll be back in two days, and I'll call you every chance I get."

"Okay. Please be safe and call me. Now give me some kisses!"

I had a ten-minute drive to work, so I grabbed my duffle bag and hit the road. It was the same as every other day; busy and crowded. It was also the weekend, and a lot of people took trips Friday-Monday. I went to the back and clocked in.

"Good morning, Azia. How's your morning going?" my coworker greeted me.

"It's going good, Tracey. How about yours?"

"Ouu, I had the best night, girl. I'll tell you about it on the plane."

"You're going with me today?"

"Yes. Samantha called off. She's been feeling sick for the last two days."

"I hope she feels better. I'll see you on the plane. I have to go to the restroom."

Tracey was an older lady, and she didn't hold back her voice for anything. She'll tell you how it is whether you liked it or not. I had to get used to her. Samantha worked with me the majority of the time. I believed she and one of the pilots had something going on.

"So, girl, let me tell you. My ex-husband came over last night, and it went down." Tracey came to the back of the plane and sat next to me.

"Ouuu, Ms. Tracey, you are a bad girl."

"Last night, I was the robber, and he was the copper."

"You can't be making me laugh that loud with passengers on the plane."

"It was amazing, girl. I guess he thought I was gon' take his cheating ass back. Nope, I just wanted some dick last night."

"Naw, we don't do the cheaters, Ms. Tracey."

"When I was done, I sent his ass back home to his wife."

"Yesss, that's how you do it."

We got up to pass out the food and beverages and collect the trash. This guy on the plane kept staring at me, and it was kind of weird. I kept my eye on him while continuing to do my job. Wanting to get a good look at his face, I headed toward him. It was a good thing the person sitting in front of him wanted some snacks and something to drink. The man was light skinned with a low haircut. He had on a black coat and some Timberlands. When he looked at me and smiled, I smiled back, not wanting to seem rude.

Finally, the pilot announced our descent, and we returned to our stations. Today, I was happy to be working in the back of the aircraft.

"Excuse me, miss."

I turned around from wiping down the seat, and it was that dude. "Yes, may I help you with something?"

"You can start by telling me your name."

"Why would I do that?"

"I get it. You're shy. My name is Rock. I wanted to get your number, so I can call you."

"I wish I could, but I'm in a relationship. Sorry."

"Oh yeah? That's cool. We can be friends."

"Excuse me, sir. You can't be here. Did you leave something?" Tracey came and rescued me.

"No, I didn't. I'll be leaving, and I'll see you around." He pointed at me.

He was actually cute, but I wasn't about to give in. After finished cleaning the plane, Tracey and I decided to get something to eat in the airport. I called my mom to let her know I was safe and I would be home tomorrow afternoon. I also called Kameila and made sure she was straight. She found a job and had been working like crazy. The last person I called was D'Metrius, and he didn't answer, so I left a message.

"What's wrong, Azia? Are you okay?"

"Yeah, Tracey, I'm fine."

I was just wondering what the hell D'Metrius could be doing that kept him from answering the phone. I called back two more times, and still the same thing. Finally, I left it alone and ate my loaded French fries until it was time to take off again.

Wayne

"You and that bitch gon' get fucked up. Watch and see what I tell you."

Messy ass Rosalina was on the phone, yelling for no reason. She was mad because I had Kameila around JR. As long as she wasn't a threat to him, he was good. So, I sat there and let her ramble on speakerphone. D'Metrius was over, and he was cracking up; he thought this shit was funny. I wasn't about to deal with her shenanigans today, though.

"Listen, I don't feel like hearing that shit today. Either you gon' bring my son tonight or not."

"I'll think about it."

Click!

"Yo, Rosalina is a trip."

"Nigga, who you telling? The shit she was saying didn't even make sense."

We were at my house, trying to come up with a plan to take down Dhillon. He had been on our ass for the last two days. He kept calling D and telling him he needed to watch his people because our time was coming to an end. See, he still didn't know we killed his son and knew who his daughter was, but we would use that to our advantage soon enough.

"Man, my phone has been on silent all this time, and Azia called me four times. I know she's going to be pissed that I didn't answer."

"Just leave her a message, letting her know what happened."

"In the meantime, we need to figure some shit out because this nigga got to go."

"Let's do a trial run. Me and you go to Miami. We can take Andrew and text him when the coast is clear to set up the cameras. We can tell him that we know where his son and daughter are."

"We gon' do part of that, bro. Let's go talk to Andrew."

I didn't know what this nigga had up his sleeve, but he was smiling. On the way to Drew's house, I called Kameila to see if she could come over tonight. I didn't know if this girl knew some type of voodoo or what, but I wasn't leaving her anytime soon. Her spirit was just so bright. She wasn't into drama, and I liked that. I was thinking about giving her a key, so I wouldn't have to keep going downstairs to open the door.

"Yo, Andrew, I need your help with something. You know how to tap phones?" D asked when we pulled up on Drew.

"I can do anything you need me to."

"Tap this number for me. I need some information if we about to take him out the game."

After we got the information, we left. Drew would keep us posted on any deliveries. We weren't trying to be reckless this time. We needed to think some things through, and we had two weeks to put this plan in motion.

D dropped me off at home, and I felt bad for my nigga. He was still upset that Azia had called, and he missed it. When I walked into my house, I felt like turning around and walking the fuck back out.

"Hey, baby, where you coming from?"

Now I knew damn well this muthafucka didn't have a key to my house. She was getting crazier and crazier by the day.

"Why are you in my house, sitting on my damn couch?" I asked Rosalina.

"I cooked you dinner, and I wanted to chill with you and JR tonight."

"How did you get in here, let alone cook dinner?"

"You know I have my ways, hubby. Now come in and get comfortable."

Yes, that's another secret that I hadn't told Kameila. I had been married for four years and trying to divorce her for the last year. We were happy the first year and a half of our marriage, but when I found out she cheated on me, I was done. I was paying all the bills and taking care of her before she got pregnant. When I found out, I was still there, even though it was a possibility that the baby wasn't mine.

"You need to sign those papers, so I don't have to deal with you unless it has to do with JR."

"You know I want to work it out, and I still love you, Wayne. Why do you still treat me like this?"

"You put us through this, not me. I was doing my part while you were creeping."

"How many times do I have to apologize? Wayne, I was in a dark place at that time. You know I lost my father, and my mother wasn't shit. You were busy ripping and running the streets, and he was there to console me."

"You saying ripping and running like I was out fucking bitches and not making money for us. Not just me, Rosalina, but us. You weren't worried about that, though. You could've gotten a job or went back to school, but you didn't. That was your choice. You wanted to shop 'til you drop and shit."

"Listen, I didn't come over here to argue. I just want to relax with my husband and son."

I went upstairs to my bedroom and locked the door. This muthafucka was crazy, and I didn't have time for her ass. Kameila was supposed to come over tonight, but now that Rosalina was there, that wasn't happening. I turned the shower on after I rolled up this wood. I barely smoked weed, but when I was stressed, I had a stash to smoke from.

After I got out of the shower, I put on some basketball shorts and sat on the edge of the bed. I picked up the lighter and was about to light this wood when I heard, "Bitch, why are you here?"

I ran downstairs, and Kameila was standing at the door.

"Kameila..."

That was all I could get out before she hit me upside my head with her purse. I grabbed the side of my head and noticed that Kameila had tears coming from her eyes. At that point, I knew Rosalina had told her about being my wife.

Kameila walked out the door, and I ran after her, but she hopped in her car and pulled off. I felt so bad that she had found out this way. Rosalina had to get the fuck on, and I meant now. JR was asleep, and I wasn't about to wake him up.

"Get the fuck out of my house, now! All you do is start shit, and I'm tired of it."

"It was time she knew the truth. I spared her feelings the first time I saw her."

"Yeah, okay. Just get your shit, including your dinner, and leave."

Rosalina huffed and puffed as she grabbed her purse. When she tried to get JR, I stopped her. She slammed the door, and he started crying. I picked him up and rocked him back to sleep for like twenty minutes, then I called the pizza place and ordered some food.

I turned on the TV and watched ESPN for the remainder of the night. I tried calling Kameila, but of course, I didn't get an answer. That made me even more pissed.

Kameila

I hadn't seen nor heard from Wayne in three weeks. The fact that he had sex with the same bitch who I had just fought was beyond me. Granted, that was his baby mother or whatever, but we were together so that shit was bold as hell. I couldn't do no cheating shit, and I wasn't about to go through it either. I had dealt with that shit from my ex, and I promised myself that I would not go through that in another relationship. That shit was dead.

"Are you ready, ma'am? While you over there daydreaming," Azia said as she walked into my house

"Yes, I'm ready. And I wasn't daydreaming."

"Yeah, so that smile while scrolling through those text messages wasn't nothing, huh?"

"Damn, bitch, you're a little nosey this afternoon."

We laughed.

Azia was my girl, and I would go to war for her. She had never crossed me, and I would never cross her. Real friends are hard to come by, and she was definitely one to keep. We were on our way to the nail shop and to get some lunch. Since we'd both been working, we hadn't spent any time together. I had been working for the postal service for a month, and I loved it. The neighborhood that I delivered mail in was decent—mostly older people and nice little dogs. I had been saving my checks so I could apply for a cannabis license, which would cost five thousand dollars.

"You know I'm nosey. You should be used to that by now."

"I was going through Wayne's text messages. I miss him, but I can't deal with no cheater."

"Maybe you should call him. You know she didn't like you from the jump. She probably was lying, girl. You know how these baby mothers get."

"That may be true, but he came downstairs with no shirt on and some basketball shorts. She answered the door in her bra and panties."

"Oh, see, you didn't tell me that part. We can whoop his ass. You know I'm down." She giggled.

"Of course, but that doesn't make it any better."

"Yeah, you're right."

My cousin had opened her own nail salon called Pretty Me. It wasn't that far from us, and I will always support her. She was the only family member I really got along with. My cousin had a husband and a daughter, so she was not into drama. The line was wrapped around the corner, and I didn't feel like standing in it, but she was family, and I had nothing else to do at that moment.

"Girl, my stomach is in my back. I'm so hungry," Azia said.

"You've been eating since we left the house. Is it something you want to tell me?" I asked.

"Girl, bye. I'm good over here."

"Wayne is calling me. Should I answer?"

"If you want to talk to him, go ahead."

I decided against it. I'd probably call him back later once I was settled at home. I wasn't sure what was gonna happen, but I would wait until later. Ten people had left the line, complaining about the wait, so that moved us up. About an hour went past before we were finally in the door and seated. The salon was so nice! She had mirrors on every wall, beautiful massage chairs for the pedicures, and all the nail polishes were displayed so nicely on the walls.

"Oh, yeah, this is about to be the new nail spot. It's so beautiful."

"I was just thinking the same thing. It's so dope."

"Hey, ladies, my name is Porsha, and I want to welcome you to Pretty Me Nails. I hope you enjoy our complimentary wine and fruit. Thanks for letting our team get you pretty," the receptionist introduced herself. This was a great setting.

"Hey, loves, so glad y'all made it. I'll have Teresa and

Lynn come and get y'all together," my cousin walked up and said.

"You knew we were coming. We can't miss your special day," Azia said.

"And I appreciate y'all. Let's get pretty!"

We were there for two hours getting manis and pedis. We got our eyebrows done and lashes too. I felt pretty, and I was starving. I couldn't wait to get to this burger place. Azia was on the phone with D'Metrius, and I was jealous. I wanted to talk to Wayne, but I couldn't pull myself together to call him.

"Damn, everywhere we've gone so far has been crowded, and it's a weekday," Azia complained.

"I really wanted Portillo's, but that line... I just couldn't do it," I told her.

"Well, we should've stayed because there goes Wayne and his son."

I turned around so fast, and there he was, looking all scrumptious. My first instinct was to run up to him and give him a hug, but I stayed put. I buried my face in the menu, so I wouldn't see him or the other way around. Of course, if he saw Azia, he'd know I wasn't far.

"What up, y'all?" Wayne walked over, and D'Metrius wasn't far behind. That made me wonder if Azia had set this shit up. She *was* all giggly on the phone while talking to his ass in the car, now that I thought about it.

When I looked up, she was smiling. That's when I knew she had been talking to them all this time.

"You're not speaking to me, Kameila?"

"Hi, Wayne," I said and started playing with JR.

We ordered our food, and while we waited for it to come, I scrolled through my social media. I had a DM from this guy named Kyle. He was cute, and I could use someone to talk to. I hadn't been talking to anyone, so this would be a start. I wrote him back, and we were writing to each other when Wayne took my phone and put it in his pocket.

"Can you give me my phone back, sir?" I snapped.

"We all over here conversing, and you just in yo' phone, texting other niggas."

"Nobody said nothing when you was fucking that bitch three weeks ago."

"Fuck are you talking about?"

"Act stupid if you want to. Give me my phone."

He acted crazy and didn't give me my phone back, so I just waited until my food came. While I was eating, Azia came and sat next to me. She told me he probably wasn't lying. I didn't give a fuck at that point; I just wanted my shit and to go back home. I was already pissed that she had invited them and didn't even warn me.

Wayne walked over and put my phone on the table. "I didn't have sex with her. She was trying to make you mad."

"I figured that, but her being in her bra and panties is a problem for me."

"You're just not listening to anything I'm saying, are you? She did all that shit on purpose when she saw you getting out of your car."

Somebody was staring out the window when I pulled up, but I thought it was his son. She did all that shit because she knew he liked me. This was one miserable bitch, but I was gon' show her how to play this game the right way.

Meka

Five months had passed since my mother's death. It still hurt like crazy, and some days, I couldn't bear the pain. I invited my brother to come over for dinner, and I made his favorite meal, corned beef, cabbage, mac and cheese, and cornbread muffins. I had moved into the house that Lucus asked me to look at, and it was perfect for us. It was a four-bedroom, three-and-a-half bath. We had a basketball court outside because he wanted to start back playing ball.

Just as I was taking the mac and cheese out of the oven, my phone rang. I set the pan on the counter and picked it up.

"Hey, beautiful, what are you doing?" Lucus said.

"I'm finishing up the food."

"Okay, I'll be home soon."

Lucus had gone to get his hair cut, and he took his

141

nephew with him. His brother had to work and couldn't find his baby mother. Lucus said she always does that and turns back up two days later. I had one hour to get ready, so I turned the shower on then picked out some leggings and a shirt to wear.

After I showered and got dressed, I went downstairs to set the table for dinner. I had just finished mixing a batch of my famous champagne punch when the doorbell rang.

"What up, sis? It smells so good in here," Metri said as he gave me a hug.

"Now, you know I can throw down when I want to."

"Of course. This is my girl, Azia. You remember her, right?"

"I do. It's nice to see you again."

When I first met Azia, we didn't have a good start. I was trying to feel her out, but it came across in a negative way. She seemed cool, though. This was only the second girl my brother had brought around the family. The first girl lied about being pregnant, and he found out about it, so that was a wrap. She said she was scared to lose him, but she had to know a baby would not keep a man who didn't want to be kept. He was younger at the time and was running the streets non-stop. Metri was a bit reckless back then, but he had been doing better over the last three years.

"Same here. I know we didn't have a good start last time, but I plan to change that."

"Yes, girl. I had to feel you out and see where your head was."

"I understand. I'd probably be the same way if I had an older brother," she said, and we laughed.

I showed them around the house, and as soon as we made it back to the living room, Lucus and his nephew walked through the door. After speaking to everyone, Lucus put the drinks in the kitchen. He looked like he was upset, and I wondered what was wrong.

"Lucus, are you alright?"

"Yeah, I'm good. I just got a lot on my mind. We have company, so we can talk later."

"We can go upstairs, and you can tell me what's going on," I insisted.

He walked up the stairs, and I followed suit.

"My brother got shot today, walking into his job. He's in critical condition, and we don't know if he's going to make it."

"Oh, my god! Baby, I'm so sorry to hear that. Do y'all have any idea of who could've done it?"

"Honestly, I believe it was his baby mother. They were going through custody issues, and she wasn't complying with the rules. She would barely bring Kace over when she was supposed to. This is just so fucked up." Lucas sat on the edge of the bed and put his head in his hands.

I wrapped my arms around him and kissed the top of his head. "I'm here for anything you need, baby. Give me her name. Metri can have someone track her and see what's going on."

"I forgot about that. Shit, yeah, let's get on it."

We went downstairs, and Azia and Metri were playing with Kace in the living room. They were building houses with the Legos. Kace was just so happy, and I felt bad inside because he probably wouldn't see his dad again.

"Food is ready, and everyone can come sit at the dining room table."

"Meka, this food smells and looks so good. I can't wait to dig in," Azia said.

"Thank you, Azia. It's the bomb.com."

"Sis, you should open a food truck. This shit will sell like crazy."

"I was actually thinking about starting back sewing and opening a boutique."

"Ouu, that sounds nice. I've tried sewing before, but it just didn't work for me."

"It definitely takes time and patience, but I've worked on a few pieces over the last two days."

"Lucus, what's the word, man? Why are you so quiet?" Metri asked.

"I just got a lot on my mind, that's all."

"You need to go somewhere so we can talk?"

"Nah, I'll send Kace in the backroom to play with the toys."

After everyone finished eating, Azia and I cleared the table. She even helped me wash the dishes.

"So, what do you do?" I asked her.

"I'm a flight attendant at the moment."

"That's dope as hell. You like it?"

"Yes, it's a good job. I just don't like being away for days at a time. They're trying to hire me full time, but I told them I don't know just yet."

"I understand that fully, but you have to think about yourself and your future, girl. Do you like to do anything else?"

"I haven't thought about anything else."

"It's okay. You still have time to figure things out."

Azia was a very cool girl, and I could see why Metri liked her. Once the kitchen was clean, we went into the living room and turned on a movie. Metri and Lucus told us they would be right back. I already knew what was up, so I called Kace to join us in the living room.

Azia

"What are you about to do when you get off?" my co-worker, Carlee, asked.

"Run to my shower. It's been so hot today, and I've been sweating like crazy."

"Yeah, it's hot as hell, and this air conditioner is not helping."

We were on our way back to the airport, and I couldn't wait. After we left Meka's house two days ago, my boss had called me into work. Samantha couldn't make it because she was at the hospital with her daughter. She made up so many excuses, and I didn't see how she still worked there. I had been at the airline for almost five months, and I hadn't missed a day. I didn't call off because I liked money, and this job paid me very well. Whenever I got called in at the last minute, I got paid double.

"Ms. Cook, have you thought about taking the job full time?" my boss asked when we returned.

"I'm still thinking about it, Mr. Jones. I have a lot going on right now. I really think just being on call works for me at this moment."

"Your pay goes up, if that makes it any better."

"That sounds good, but I don't know just yet."

"If I don't have an answer by next week, I'll have to give it to someone else."

"I understand. I'll let you know something before the week is over."

"Okay, have a great day, and I look forward to your call."

As I walked to my car, that same dude from the airplane last week was back. I saw him walking toward me, and I started looking at my phone.

"What's up? You remember me?"

"No, who are you?"

"I'm John. I know you remember me from the plane ride last week. Where are you on your way to?"

"You mighty nosey, sir."

"I just want to know where I can meet you. I'm in town for my cousin's birthday weekend."

"That's nice, but I gotta go. My feet hurt from these heels, and I'm tired."

"So, your answer is home?"

"Yes, that's my answer. Can I go now?"

"Sure, why don't you put my number in your phone?"

"I can't, sorry. I have a man waiting for me to get home."

"I said put my number in your phone, not give me your number, shorty. You can use that number whenever you feel like it."

"If you insist."

"I'll see you around, shorty."

He walked off, and I was kind of happy, but I still wanted to talk to him. He just seemed cool as hell. I didn't know why I put his number in my phone because I would never use it. Shaking my head, I put my bag in the trunk and got in the car.

Twenty minutes later, I pulled up to my house, and I felt relieved. I couldn't wait to get in the shower and cook. I was tired of fast food; I wanted some soul food, and that's what I would cook.

"Hey, beautiful."

I was shocked to see Metri in the living room. He told me he was at Wayne's house, handling some business. He walked up and hugged me so tight. As I stared up into his eyes, he looked down at me with a smile.

"I have to get in the shower. I'm sweaty," I told him.

"Your shower is already running, and dinner is already made."

"Oou, look at you. I like it here."

I went to the shower, and it was steaming hot. The mirror was fogged up, so I knew it was just right. I grabbed my shower cap and body wash from the shelf. Standing under the water made me feel so good. I washed my face then proceeded to wash my body. After I rinsed off, I got out and grabbed my towel.

Before I could get all the way into the bedroom, Metri came and picked me up. He playfully threw me on the bed and separated my legs. His head went straight between my legs, where he started to lick my clit. At first, he went slowly, and then he sped up. He wouldn't let me move my legs, even after I came twice. Finally, he flipped me over and slapped my ass hard as hell on both cheeks. That shit made me wetter, and I started throwing my ass back as soon as his twelve inches went in. D'Metri's dick was bigger than anyone I'd ever had sex with, but I'd only had sex with three other people.

"Throw that ass back, baby," he commanded.

"You like that, baby?" I started twerking my ass cheeks one by one on his dick.

"Hell, yeah, Azia. Do that shit, baby."

The only sound in the room was our bodies slapping against each other.

"Ohhhh, fuuuckkkk," he screamed as he came.

"Oh, you were waiting on that, huh?" I laughed as I walked back into the bathroom to clean myself off again.

"You know you can't be leaving me that long."

"I was gone for three days, babe."

"My point exactly."

I waved him off and went downstairs to see what he had done in the kitchen. There was a pan of fried chicken, some greens, and mac and cheese. I made our plates, then we sat in the living room and turned on a movie.

"Who made this food? Because I know you didn't."

"Why you gotta play me like that?"

"I'm just saying, babe. I know you didn't cook this food. Who did, Meka?"

"Yeah, man, dang."

We both laughed.

I knew he had somebody cook it because this man hadn't stepped foot near a stove since we'd been in this house. He'd been with me ever since I got the house and had probably been home only about four times.

"I appreciate this to the fullest because I wanted some real food. I was tired of that fast food," I told him.

"I know how much you love your soul food." He gave me a kiss.

His phone rang, and from the face he made before he answered it, I knew it wasn't gonna be a good call.

"What up, bro?" He answered the phone then walked to the back of the house.

I texted Kameila and told her I was back and we should hang out when she's free. We texted for a minute, then D'Metrius came back, and he was upset.

"Babe, is everything good?" I asked.

"Somebody stole our shipment today, and I have to figure out what happened."

"Please be careful, babe. I don't want anything to happen to you."

"I'm good, baby. I'll be back later."

He went upstairs, and I heard the shower running. *Why would someone do that?* I wondered. I wanted D'Metri to be careful because that nigga could get reckless when he was upset. I had seen it twice, and I didn't ever want to see him that mad again.

After he left, I went upstairs and crawled under the covers. I was sleepy, and this bed was just what I needed.

Wayne

*D*amn, when it rains, it pours. I had just gotten a call from Lucus saying the product wasn't at the drop. I didn't know what happened, but somebody better find our shit. Dhillon must've had someone steal our shit because he hadn't gotten paid yet. We needed to take this nigga down like yesterday. He was fucking with my money, and that shit was not cool. I was waiting for D to pull up, so we could go to the spot and get this meeting going.

"Man, this shit is fucked up. Where the fuck was Shane and Mike?"

"I don't know, but we about to find out."

We got out of the car and walked through the door. Everyone was there except for Shane and Mike. That was even more strange.

"Nobody heard from Shane or Mike?"

"No, and their phones are going to voicemail."

My phone rang, and it was Andrew. He had some information, and we needed to get with him asap.

"Yo, Andrew said he got some information, and we need to get to him asap."

"Let's go. Meeting over, but use what you got for now. We gon' be back popping in a minute."

Speeding through traffic, I made it to this nigga's house in fifteen minutes. We hopped out of the car, and Andrew was standing on the porch already. This shit must have been important if he was waiting on the porch for us.

"What did you find?" D asked.

"I was listening to his conversation, and he said something about he got the shipment back and two guys with it. I tracked the phone, and they were right here in Chicago about two hours ago."

"You're just now telling us this, though?" D spat.

"Listen, I had to help my mother. She's very sick, and she needed to go to the hospital."

"I hope she feels better. Thanks for the information, bro," I said.

"Can you tell us where he is now?"

Drew looked on his computer and said they were back in Miami. We had to make a trip, and I didn't know how this would go. It was actually all of our fault that we owed this nigga, but still, he was playing with fire. I didn't like anybody fucking with my money. That was how I fed my family.

"We gon' have to take a trip. We got to tell the rest of the crew to suit up," D told me.

"You sure about this, bro? You know I'm down, but we don't have a plan."

"I know, bro. We gon' come up with something. I'm about to get these guns ready, and we can leave at midnight."

"Bet, I'll be ready."

I called the crew. We had added two more people, but with Ty out of commission, plus Shane and Mike gone, that only left four of us. He had way more security than we had people, and that was going to be a problem. We had some real shooters on our team, though.

I had to stop home for a minute and get my mind right. So much shit had happened within the last two weeks, and the shit didn't seem to be slowing down. I was exhausted and fed up with Dhillon and Rosalina. Speaking of Rosalina, she was parked in front of my house when I pulled up. I let out a huge sigh and got out of the car.

"Your son wanted to see you, so I brought him over."

"Why don't you use your phone anymore? You're always popping up and shit."

"So, your son can't pop up on his dad?"

"That's not the point. He's not driving, you are, so a phone call would be nice."

I picked my son up out of the car seat and walked into the house. He started smiling and jumping around when I put him on the floor. I went into the kitchen to get a bottle of water, and I gave him some cheese puffs.

"Why would you give him those, and he has on a white shirt?"

"When you gon' sign those papers, so I can be free?"

"I was hoping we could still try to figure things out."

I was sick of the same old line she kept throwing out. Kameila and I had a long talk, and I told her the truth about what was really going on. I also showed her the divorce papers that I had my lawyer draw up for me. I was ready to be with Kameila without anything holding me back, and right now, Rosa was that setback.

"Listen, what we had was good, but our time is over. I still have love for you because you're my son's mother. But I don't want to be in a relationship with you at all. You fucked that up."

"I know I cheated on you. I understand that, but around that time, we had good and bad days. We were always arguing about you being in the streets. Spencer was there for me. I vented to him, and then one thing led to another"

"You are not trying to see that it wasn't a little incident, Rosa. I was the one who recorded you walking into the hotel that night. That whole week, you had been acting strange. When you left that Saturday night, I decided to follow you. I just recorded it to have proof for when you lied about it."

Rosa didn't know that I had followed her that night and filmed her going into the hotel. I told her that someone sent it to my phone, though. After I confronted her, I told her ass I was done and went to a hotel that night.

"I have apologized a hundred times. Wayne, why can't you forgive me?"

"Listen, I'm gon' need you to sign these papers before you leave."

I picked up JR and went upstairs. When I heard the door slam, I knew she had left without signing the damn papers.

D'Metrius

"I talked to my uncle, and he's willing to help us. We can't get on the plane with our guns, so he gon' have some for us when we touch down. Also, we're using a different airline, so he can't trace us. He got too many people working at Chicago airlines. We're leaving tomorrow night at midnight."

I told everybody willing to go with us if they didn't want to, they could stay behind and find some work. Niggas were getting paid; I don't ask anyone to do shit for free because I knew how hard times felt. I had a bank account, and that bitch was full, but I was saving all my money to build me, my wife, and my kids a nice, big family home one day. I wanted about four kids, two boys and two girls, so I hoped Azia was willing to give me some babies.

"Alright, D, we gon' be ready. You know we got your back, bro."

"I hope so because this is some real shit going on, and I need all real niggas on this trip."

"D, we know you're upset. Shit, we are too. We've been handling business together, so you know me and Tee always got your back. I have three cousins that stay in Miami, and they are willing to help us too," Black said.

"Oh, fa real? That's what we need. Call them up. I need to give them some instructions on what they can do tonight."

"Hell yeah, bro. That's basically where all my family stays. I just moved here with my mom a few years back, and Tee came with us."

He pulled out his phone and called his cousin, who was willing to help in any way. I told them to watch the house tonight and see how many people come and go. I needed an accurate count because I was tired of playing with this old ass nigga. As soon as I hung up with him, my phone rang.

"Who the fuck is calling me private?" I answered.

"Oh, you must've forgotten that your time is running out. I want my fucking money, or them two thugs you had picking up your shipment is dead."

"Dhillon, why you gotta put other people in it? This between me and you, right?"

"I'll get to the source of the problem later, but in the meantime, I want my cash."

I hung up the phone. This nigga had his coming, and I would show up, guns blazing. I didn't fuck around with arguing over the phone or the internet. Muthafuckas had to talk that tough shit in my face.

"This meeting is over. Everybody go get packed, and we'll meet back here at eleven."

I dropped Wayne off at home and went to see my sister. I didn't know if Lucus told her, but I was about to let her know what was going on. Meka had been at home since she quit working at the bar. She had started back sewing and was trying to open her boutique. I was proud of her; she needed to leave that damn bar life alone.

"Hey, bro. What's going on with you?"

"You have turned the living room into the sewing room."

"No, I'm about to put this stuff up in the back room and start hanging up my designs."

"That's what's up, sis. You doing your thang, but listen, me and the crew are going to Miami to handle this nigga Dhillon. He tripping, and he got two of our men."

"What? Oh, my god, Metri! You can't go there. It's not safe. Didn't you say he has more security than you have people?"

"I got this under control, Meka. We gon' be good, and we gon' be back in one piece, I promise you."

"Lord, help me. When are y'all leaving?"

"At midnight."

"Damn, bro, this shit is crazy. I'm gon' be praying like hell. Please be careful."

"We'll be back in two days tops. Keep an eye on Azia for me. Hang out with her and get to know her better."

"Oh, you must really like her. I got you, though, bro."

"Yeah, I do, and soon, she's going to be your sister-in-law, so do what I said. I'll see you later."

I gave my sister a hug and kissed her cheek. She was crying, and I didn't know why. I promised her I'd be back, and everything would be back to normal.

After I left Meka's house, I headed home. I had an urge to take my girl out, so I gave her a call.

"Hey, baby, get dressed. I want to go out for seafood," I said when she answered.

"Ouu, now you know I like the sound of that."

"I'll be pulling up in twenty minutes, so that's enough time for your slow ass to get dressed." I laughed.

"I am not slow! I just can't walk out the house looking any kind of way."

"I know, baby, and I appreciate that. But get ready. I'm in traffic."

I made a reservation for Dina's Seafood Palace, which was usually crowded. Whenever we rode past, Azia would always say, "I want to try that place out, but that line is out the door." I didn't know how she would take the news I had to give her, but it was something I had to do.

"You're looking like the menu. I want to take you back inside," I told Azia when she walked out.

"Thanks, babe. I did my best." I loved that smile.

"You know you don't have to try very hard, baby."

"Aren't you sweet?"

It took us forty-five minutes to get to the restaurant. I

could've made it sooner, but I wasn't rushing. Instead, I was enjoying my girl smiling and grooving to the old-school music playing on the radio.

"It's not crowded today. This is so awesome. How'd you know I wanted to eat here?"

"I listen to you, baby, even when you think I'm not."

We were seated at a table near the back. Nobody could sit behind me, so that was good. The waiter handed us our menus, and Azia ordered some wine. I needed something more potent, so I ordered Hennessy. As I looked at the menu, I glanced toward the door and saw Dhillon's daughter walk in with some dude. They sat at a table by the window. I wondered if her father had her watching some shit or if she was really on a date.

Azia

As I looked at the menu, I noticed that D'Metrius kept looking at a table behind me. So, I turned around and saw that ole dude from the plane was there with the girl who D'Metrius claimed he wasn't on a date with last time. Now, I wondered why this nigga was looking at her like that when he was there with me.

"What's wrong with you?" I asked.

"Nothing, I'm good. You know what you're ordering?"

Now here this nigga goes trying to rush and eat.

"Yeah, we can order. I'm ready, but why do you keep looking at that table?"

"Listen, it's not what you think. That girl is Dhillon's daughter. I think he got them watching me or some shit. He caught two of my workers slipping when they were picking up the shipment. Today, he called and told me that he had them. Me and the crew are going to Miami tonight. We have to do something about his ass."

D'Metrius said that shit fast as hell! I barely understood what came out of his mouth. I didn't know if I could deal with this shit. He was basically going to Miami to have a shootout, and I didn't know if he would make it back alive.

"Umm, I'm trying to process this, but that dude was at the airport. He was even on the same plane as me."

"Are you serious right now? Azia, has he said anything to you?"

"Yes, he tried to talk to me, and he also put his number in my phone," I told him.

I probably shouldn't have said that last part, but it kind of just slipped out.

"We'll talk about that later. Here comes the waiter."

"Have you made your selections yet?"

"Yes, I'll have the salmon alfredo with garlic bread," I told him.

"I'll take the steak and shrimp with loaded mashed potatoes."

"Thank you, I'll put that in for you."

After he walked away, I got up and went to the restroom. That wine was running straight through me. It felt like I had been holding that pee for a long time. I had on heels, and trying to flush that toilet with one foot was hard business. I shook my head and opened the door. The girl from the table was standing next to the sink, looking at me.

"You know me or something?" I asked.

"No, and I don't care to, but your little boyfriend owes my dad some money. If he doesn't pay him by tomorrow, he's going to die."

"What the fuck you mean? Bitch, you better get out my face before I drag you with my heels on."

"Why are you upset because y'all so broke that you can't pay back the money you owe?"

"First off, I don't owe you shit. Now get the fuck out of my face. This is the last time I'm going to tell you that."

I went to the sink and washed my hands while she stood there looking crazy, but she had sense enough to keep them hands by her side.

When I walked out the door and went back to the table, D'Metrius was nowhere to be found. I searched all over the place. The dude, John, from the airport wasn't there anymore either. I went back to the restroom, and that girl was gone too. *Now what the fuck is really going on? This has got to be the worst day of all.*

"D'Metrius, where did you go? Call me when you get this message."

I had left several voicemails and asked the waiter if he'd seen him. Since I didn't have his keys, I couldn't drive the car, so I had to call an Uber to take me home. When I got home, I called him again, and he didn't answer. I called Kameila to see if she was home, but she was just getting off work. She said she'd come over once she got home. The next call I made was to D'Metrius's sister.

"Meka, can you come to my house, please? I'm about to

send you the address. It's important. It's about your brother," I said when she answered.

"What! I'm on my way."

About thirty minutes later, there was a knock on the door.

"Who is it?" I yelled.

"Meila, girl. Open up."

"Girl, D'Metrius is gone. I think Dhillon had him kidnapped or worse."

"What the fu—"

Before she could finish, Meka walked through the door.

"What's going on? What happened to my brother?"

I told them about this evening and what happened at the restaurant, including the bathroom scene. Meka looked so scared, and I was right along with her. She called Wayne, and he was on his way over. This was so fucked up and scary. I didn't know what to do.

"I need you to tell me one more time what happened, so I can fully understand where to go from here," Wayne said.

"We had gone to Dina's, and the girl he went to dinner with a couple of weeks ago walked through the door with this dude I had seen at the airport. I went to the restroom, and I had a couple of words with the girl. When I went back to the table, D'Metrius was gone, and so was ole boy."

"Do you have any information about this guy?" Wayne asked.

"I have a number that he put in my phone when he tried to talk to me," I confessed.

"We'll talk about that later. Call the number and see what happens."

I called the number, and it went straight to voicemail. When I tried again, it rang like five times, but the same thing happened.

"Listen, I got this dude who can track both of their numbers. I'll be back with some information," Wayne said.

"Oh, no, you don't. We are all coming with you. We want to know what's going on."

"Listen, this shit isn't safe, and if you don't know what you're doing, stay ya ass here."

We all got up and followed Wayne to his truck. Once we got in, he pulled off. He made a call to some dude named Andrew and told him he was on the way. Wayne was speeding through traffic, running red lights, and almost hit the back of somebody's car. Thankfully, we made it there in one piece.

"Trace these two numbers for me and see what you come up with. D is missing, and I believe this nigga had something to do with it. I need this information like yesterday. How long will it take?" Wayne said to Andrew as soon as we arrived.

"Give me thirty minutes to an hour, and I should have something."

"Bet."

"Man, I wish we could see the videotape from tonight. I know they have cameras," I said.

"Bingo. Is the manager a man or lady?" Wayne responded.

"A man. He's a little older, probably fifty-something."

"You down to try and seduce him? Maybe he'll give in if he thinks he's about to get something out of the deal," he suggested.

"Hell yeah, let's go."

Meka called Lucus and told him what was going on. He passed the message to the other guys, and everyone was tripping out.

"So, the dude John, I remember he got in a silver BMW with a light skinned dude who had dreads. The license plate is 2dpe4u," I said.

"Too dope for you... that sounds like Dhillon, the description and all. This nigga had to have been here all this time. We have to lay low and figure something out because he could come after one of us soon," Wayne said.

My phone rang, and it was my mom. She sounded scared as hell. I told them we had to make a detour to her house. When we pulled up, the door was already open, and the house was trashed. Somebody had spray-painted the walls too.

"Mom, what happened?"

"I don't know. When I got home, the door was open, and I saw this, so I called you."

I shook my head and looked at Wayne. All I could do was cry. Everything was going so well, and now everything was bad as hell. This had to be some shit that Dhillon nigga was up to, and he fucked with my mother's house.

"Ma, everything is going to be okay. I'll clean this up tomorrow. In the meantime, come to my house, and you'll be safe," I told her.

"What is going on here, Azia? I want answers now."

"I'll explain everything on the way to my house, I promise."

I went upstairs and packed my mom a bag. Thankfully, they didn't do anything to the upstairs. As I walked back down the stairs, I saw a piece of paper. When I read it, I was stuck.

"This letter says he wants his money in two hours, or we're all dead," I told everyone.

"Andrew is calling. Let's drop your mother off, so we can go," Wayne said.

This was giving me a headache.

After dropping my mama off and telling her a short version of the issue, she was slightly satisfied. This was about to be a very long night.

Wayne

I talked the ladies into staying at Azia's house with her mom. They agreed because they didn't want anything to happen to her. This was about to be a very long night, but I wouldn't stop looking for these niggas. They had D, Shane, and Mike. How the hell all these niggas get caught slipping, especially D? That wasn't him. Something had to have happened. Then I thought about the restaurant they were at. Dina's Seafood Palace: it sounded like something was up with that.

"What up, Drew? You got something for me?"

I hopped out of the truck and started walking toward the porch. He was always sitting on the porch, observing everything with a Heineken in his hand.

"Both phones are untraceable. I've been trying, and I can't get anything."

"Damn, man! Alright, I need to check out some cameras at that restaurant."

"Let me know if you need me. D is like my brother too."

"You can hack these cameras for me. I'll distract them, and you do what you have to."

"Let's go."

Drew grabbed his bag with his computer, and we hopped in the truck. The place was twenty minutes from Drew's house. I tried calling D's phone just to see if he would answer and tell us he was playing around. It rang, but he didn't answer. Now that was strange because Drew said both phones were going to voicemail.

"I just called his phone. It rang, but he didn't answer."

"Let me try to trace it again."

"We're here. Are you ready?"

"Always, but his phone says it's here somewhere."

"Are you fucking serious? That means you better strap up, homeboy. I'm about to call the crew because if his phone is here, so is he."

"Oh, you already know I stay ready." He showed his two desert eagles on both his sides.

Walking up to the building, I looked around at the parked cars. The same car that Azia described was parked in the first space. Andrew walked over and put a tracking device underneath it. We then walked into the restaurant and asked for the manager.

"Hello, sir, how may I assist you today?"

"I have a question. My brother came in here yesterday, and he hasn't been back home. Have you seen him?"

"We have a lot of people coming and going. Can you describe him for me?"

"Where is the restroom?" Andrew asked.

"It's right around that corner."

I didn't know what he was up to, but I knew he'd find out something. I described D to the manager and even described Azia. He said he wasn't working last night, so he couldn't tell me anything. That was lie number one because I asked Azia what the manager looked like, and she described his ass.

"Are you lying to me? Because I hate liars, sir."

"Is everything alright out here, Mr. Juke?" a server came out and asked.

"Yes. He's looking for his brother who was at the restaurant yesterday but didn't make it back home."

"Oh, sorry, we can't help you." The server had me suspicious of her ass now because she had walked past at first, then she came back and asked him if everything was okay.

"You can, and you will."

Andrew came back from the restrooms with a smile on his face. I already knew he had some information, and we needed to go.

"I found one of the cameras, and I was able to download the footage."

"How the hell did you do that in ten minutes, Drew?"

"There's a camera in the hallway before you get to the

bathroom. I just hooked my cord in and downloaded that tape. To my surprise, it was more on there than I thought."

We watched the video while we were still in the parking lot. The footage showed D and Azia sitting at the table, and we also saw when Dhillon's daughter walked in with the John dude. We saw Azia and D have some words, and then Azia got up and went toward the restroom.

"This doesn't tell us shit, man. Thought you had something," I told Drew.

"Keep watching."

The camera then cut to the parking lot, and I saw D walk to his car and get something out. A van pulled up right when he closed the car door, and some niggas jumped out. One hit him in the head with a gun, then they tossed him in the van and peeled out.

"Everyone in this restaurant has to go. We gon' come back tonight," I told Drew.

"Me and my crew will meet you here. What time?"

"Okay, Drew with the crew, be back here at eleven. That's what time they close."

"Remember, we have a tracker on that car. That'll give us information too."

"Bet."

I dropped Drew back off and called Meka to see where they were. She said they were still at Azia's house. I told them everything that happened and about what we saw on the video. Then, I headed home so I could get the rest of the things I needed.

When I pulled up at home, there was a car seat on the porch with an orange envelope on top of it.

"Now, why would your mama leave you out here and not call me?"

This bitch done left my son on the porch, strapped in his seat, with the divorce papers on top of him. I hurriedly unlocked the door, so he could get some heat. It wasn't freezing outside, but it was cold enough for a child to get sick. I called Rosa's phone, and it went straight to voicemail, so I left her a message and told her she better not ever show her face over there again. I was so glad she signed those papers, though. Now I was free from her for good. The problem was, I still had shit to handle, and I couldn't take JR with me, so I called my aunt.

"Hey, Auntie, sorry about the late notice, but could you please watch JR for me? I need to handle some business right quick."

"Of course! Bring his little handsome self over here. I just made some chocolate chip cookies."

"That's so sweet. I'll bring him in another hour."

"Okay, baby."

My auntie loved my son. We were the only family members who really kept in contact with each other. When my mother passed away, I stayed with my auntie until I started doing shit on my own. I got my own house at twenty, but I always called and gave her money so she would be straight, and she knew she could call me anytime, and I was coming.

When we got to my aunt's house, the smell of fresh-baked cookies made my stomach rumble. I headed straight to the kitchen and snagged a few before I got ready to leave.

"I'm not sure what time I'll be done, Auntie, but I'll call you."

"Boy, it's already ten-thirty. Come pick him up in two days. We are about to hang out. Go have fun. I hope you're going on a date."

"Nah, it's just business for real. I love you, and I'll call y'all tomorrow."

"Okay, be careful. Love you too."

It was already ten forty-five, and I literally had fifteen minutes to get to the restaurant. I had to get on the express-way, and thank God it wasn't crowded. I was at the restaurant in ten minutes, and I saw Andrew's car parked down the street. That BMW was still in the same spot.

"What are we doing?"

I turned around, and the girls were standing right there with pistols in front of them. I didn't even have to ask where they got the guns from. D made sure his sister was strapped, especially because she was working at the bar.

Meka

After Wayne called and told me what happened, I told Azia and Kameila. That was my brother out there, so I was going to help. I knew how to shoot all kinds of guns because my brother had taught me some shit about this life. He knew if he was in it, I would be right by his side. I didn't do the drops and shit, but I would help the crew out if they needed a shooter.

"Azia and Kameila, do y'all know how to shoot guns?" I had to whisper because her mother was in the back room, and I was quite sure she was listening.

"Yup, I do," Kameila said.

"Actually, D'Metrius taught me how to shoot almost three weeks ago, and he bought me a gun," Azia added.

"That's good because I'm going to help Wayne try to find Metri. If we find him, we might be able to find the other two men they have as well."

"Umm, I don't know about this. I want to help because it's D'Metrius, but I'm also scared of getting shot," Azia said.

"Listen, this is part of the game. Sometimes the women have to step out of their shells and help. Whether it's a drop-off, pick up, or shooting."

"Yeah, girl, I can't stand Wayne's ass right now, but I'm down to help," Kameila added.

"Welp, that's two of us. What you gon' do?" I turned to Azia and asked.

"Fuck it, I'm down. What are we doing?"

"Let's get dressed. We'll discuss that on the way," I told her.

I called Lucus to see what time they were going back to the place. He told me at 11:00, and I told him to be careful. He didn't know that we were showing up—no one did—but we were gon' be there and ready for whatever.

"We have to be there at eleven. It's ten now, and I need to go home right fast," I announced.

"Alright, we can put our stuff on at your house," Kameila said.

They grabbed their bags, and we headed out.

"Ma, I'll be back later. I locked all the doors and the windows," Azia told her mother.

"Okay, baby, be careful. I know how to protect myself. I got Betty right beside me."

I looked at her, and we all burst out laughing. Azia's mom was hilarious. This was my first time hanging with Azia and really meeting Kameila. They were actually cool ass people. Azia was a little scared, I could tell, but she was trying to maintain her composure. I understood all of that. She wasn't into this lifestyle, but since Metri was her man, she wanted to help. Kameila, on the other hand, was on her game. I didn't know her history, but she seemed to know what she was doing.

"No cars are out here," Kameila said when we pulled up to the restaurant.

"They'll be pulling up shortly. They're not really the on time type of people."

I parked down the street, but we could see the building. Some dude walked out, looked around, and went back in. I told the ladies to get ready, and we said a little prayer before getting out of the car.

"What are we about to do?" I asked.

Wayne turned around and was shocked to see us standing there with our guns. I wasn't playing. You fucking with my brothers, you fucking with me. I just wondered what Metri was going through. Like, were they beating him with different objects? This just wasn't sitting right with me, and I couldn't lose him to the streets. That was my worst fear.

"What the hell are y'all doing here?" Wayne asked.

"You know when it comes to Metri and you, I'm down for whatever. That's her man, and you're Kameila's man. Y'all need help, and we're here to do that."

"Okay, listen. We'll be going in through the back door. They have an alarm pad, but Andrew broke through that.

We're looking for a basement or some rooms, maybe even an upstairs."

We crept to the back door, where Andrew and two more guys met us. Lucus looked at me with a surprised expression. I just smiled. He should've known when I asked him what time they would be there that I was gon' show up.

"Now, listen, when we get in here, we have to split up. Lucus, you go with the ladies, and I'll go with Andrew and his team."

"Bet," everyone said at the same time.

We heard some people talking when we made it inside, but we couldn't really make out what was being said. To the left of me were some stairs, and to the right was a bathroom. We all decided to go downstairs and check it out. It was a restaurant, so everything on that floor was basically food-related.

"Look, it's three doors down here. Two people take on one," Wayne stated.

There was a lock on the door, so I pulled the hairpin out of my bun and started picking the lock. When I finally got the door open, my eyes lit up like Christmas morning. There was so much dope in there, and I was definitely taking some. I could flip this shit and get a new car and some nice boobs.

"Damn, this is their stash place, so that means D might not even be here," Lucus said.

We walked out that door and went to find Wayne and the other people. They came back around the corner and said nothing was in here. I told them about the stash room, and of course, we were going to take what we could get away with.

"Somebody's coming. We need to hide now," Wayne said.

We all ran through the door across from the stash room, and we were so quiet that you could hear a mouse pissing on cotton. I heard what sounded like two sets of footsteps coming down the stairs, and that's when I remembered we didn't close the door back.

"Yo, you left the door open?" a male voice said.

"Hell, nah. I haven't been down here. This is my first time."

"Fuck it. Let's just put this shit in these bags and go back upstairs," the first male voice responded.

Azia's phone rang. She tried to silence it, but it was too late. We got really quiet when we heard footsteps pass the door. I slipped my silencer on my gun and was prepared to kill those two niggas.

"Who the fuck are y'all?" one of the men said.

"We're not here for no problems. We were just looking for my brother," I told them.

"Why would your brother be down here?"

"Somebody kidnapped him, and I believe y'all know what's going on."

"Aye, you the lady from the plane," the guy said to Azia.

"You know me and my nigga. Now where the fuck he at?"

One of the dudes pulled out his gun, and before he

could do anything, he had one to his head. The second nigga ran up the stairs, and we knew what was about to happen. We grabbed the two bags that they had packed up and darted up the stairs. A herd of footsteps seemed to be coming toward us, but we were out the door before they could catch up. We heard gunshots, but we kept going to the car.

"Look, y'all, I think Metri's phone is right here on the ground," I said. It was cracked up, but maybe we could get some information from it.

When I looked up, I noticed his car was parked in the lot. We opened the doors but couldn't find the keys. Wayne came over, lifted the dashboard, and grabbed the extra set of keys. He drove the car back to his house, and we followed him. Fuck this restaurant! My brother wasn't there.

Kameila

ow, this is the shit I didn't sign up for. Don't get me wrong, I was far from scared. My dad taught me how to shoot at an early age. He was part of this lifestyle, too, at one point, which is why I knew so much about this game. I told Azia back when we first started dealing with them that they were drug dealers. She didn't believe me, though. She wanted to believe that D'Metrius was using the money from the insurance policy left by his mom. That may have been true, but I knew what I knew. Now she was stressed because we couldn't find D. I felt her pain, though.

"Hey, girl, it's going to be alright. D will be back in your arms in no time."

"This shit is scary. I wouldn't wish this on anyone."

Azia hadn't been answering her phone for work, and I really believed she had mentally quit. She barely cleaned her house; I had to bring her food and everything. It had been two days, and she was tripping out more and more.

"Bitch, listen here. What we're not about to do is stay in this bed any longer. It smells like ass juice in here. You need to get up and get in the shower. No, scratch that, the bathtub. I'll change your sheets and clean your room while you're doing that."

"It does not smell like booty juice, bitch."

Azia got up and went to start the water for her bath. She took her phone and something to put on. I went to the linen closet and grabbed her sheets along with a new comforter. Her room wasn't messy; she just had food bags and cups everywhere. I had just finished straightening up when she came out of the bathroom.

"When was the last time you cooked? You gon' be fat as hell, eating out all the time."

"Girl, I've been craving some steaks. I want to cook some."

We went downstairs, turned on the speaker in the kitchen, and started cleaning.

"You need to call your job and let them know you're having an issue right now before they fire yo' ass," I told Azia.

"I had ten vacation days, and I have two left, so I'll be good. I told them that I had a family emergency."

"Oh, okay, 'cause I was wondering."

"It's some steaks in the freezer. Can you pull them out, please?"

I went to the kitchen and pulled out the steaks, some asparagus, and white rice. Then I put all her dirty dishes in the dishwasher. Azia's house was never dirty; she just had little shit that needed to be done. It started smelling good after I lit two of her candles from Bath and Body Works. I was going to chill with my girl today, watch movies, and talk. My friend had been in and out for the past week, and I missed her.

I finally got back with Wayne three days ago when he showed me the divorce papers. He apologized for everything and especially him keeping the fact that he was married from me. That's why the bitch was doing all that extra shit. She had the nerve to leave her son on the front porch of his house. That shit was wild as hell.

"How do you feel now that you're back with Wayne?" Azia asked.

"Girl, the same as before. I like him, and I'm worried about him. He went to Miami with the crew, and I haven't talked to him yet."

They left for Miami this morning. Wayne figured if he couldn't find D at the restaurant, they had to have taken him to Miami. I had to work this week, and I couldn't afford to take off. I told Azia she needed to clear her head because everyone would be back in one piece. I didn't know that for sure, but I hoped I was right.

"I just want him and D to come back home soon. I miss him, girl. I think I even love the nigga."

"Yeah, same here, sis. I don't know what these niggas did to us, but we stuck."

We laughed, and then she went into the kitchen to start cooking while I turned on LMN. That was our favorite station to watch. I loved the crazy stories, and we were always yelling at the screen. My phone rang, and it was from a private number. I picked it up, and all I heard was, "Bitch, I'm coming for you," and then it hung up.

"Why are you looking crazy all of a sudden?" Azia asked.

"Girl, I think Wayne's baby mother/ex-wife just called my phone."

"What? Why?"

"You know she's still mad about us. Plus, she had to sign the divorce papers. She doesn't have her son, and she thinks I'm to blame."

"Girl, fuck her. She should've done her job as a wife, then they'd still be together."

"True."

We were watching *Stalked by My Patient* when we heard three knocks on the door. Without hesitation, we both pulled out our guns. We kept them close to us at all times. With everything going on, we had to be safe.

"What's up, ladies? I have two bottles of Stella Rosa."

"Hey, Meka. You're right on time. I have four steaks cooking, some asparagus, and white rice."

This was an unexpected guest, but she was a joy to have around. Meka was actually cooler than the first time I met her when I had to cuss her ass out. She had apologized to us both and explained that she just wanted to see where our heads were.

Azia made the plates, and Meka grabbed the wine glasses, then we were all set. Sitting in the dining room, we all were quiet for at least five minutes.

"We should go to Miami with the fellas and help them get Metri and the other guys," Meka said.

"Umm, I don't know about that. I think the fellas should hold this one down," Azia stated.

"Yeah, I don't know, Meka. I have to work, and I can't afford to lose my job," I added.

"I understand what you're saying, Meila, but Azia, you were down the first time. So, what's the difference now?"

"I like my life, and I'm not trying to lose it. Metri said there was a lot of security there. It's only like ten people with us."

"Okay, you have a point. I just thought I might run it past y'all because I'm going. I got the information out of Lucus's phone, and I'm on the next flight."

"Well, you be careful, girl. That's a crazy game."

I wasn't about to risk my life anymore for their asses. If Wayne was my husband, then we'd be having a different conversation. I had already risked my life the first time, but I wasn't letting my best friend do that shit alone. She said she wasn't going this time, and I was happy to hear that.

"Thanks for the food, ladies. It was delicious, but I have to head to the airport before I miss this flight."

"Alright, Meka. Text one of us when you land."

"Will do."

Meka left, and Azia turned to me. "Do you think I made the wrong decision, Mei?"

"Hell no! Did you hear what I told her? Them niggas are not our husbands. If they were, then that would be a different story. I'm not about to lose my job or my life over a nigga that I'm just fucking. They knew how this game went from jump street. Yeah, we went last time, but that was the first and last for me."

"Yeah, you're right. I just feel kind of bad because I don't know what he's going through. I miss him like crazy, but I don't want to die trying to find out information."

"Listen, sis, that's his sister, and those are his boys. They have known him longer than y'all have been together. He wouldn't want you out there shooting shit up or even getting shot. You have your mother to think about too. Trust me, you made the right decision," I assured her.

Azia hugged me, and we started cleaning up the dining room. She was sad and confused, but I was right there to help her. I didn't want her to feel bad because she didn't go. It wasn't her problem that her nigga owed someone money. D'Metrius had big bread, and he could've paid that shit. Instead, he refused, so now he had to deal with the consequences.

"Take a ride with me to my house. I need to check on it and grab a few things," I asked Azia.

"Let me grab my purse and lock the door," she said.

My house was literally ten minutes from there. I had to

work tomorrow, so I needed to grab my work clothes and some underwear. Today was a chill day, and I was cool with that, especially since my life had been so hectic over the past two weeks. I was concerned about Wayne, and I wanted him to be good and come back in one piece. I had also been talking to the guy who wrote to me on my page. He wanted to take me out for dinner tomorrow, but I didn't know. People on the internet were weird as hell nowadays, and I watched too much TV.

Azia came back downstairs without her purse. "Your house isn't that far. I'll just stay here. I'm really not in the mood," she told me.

"Are you sure? You were just going to get your purse."

"Yeah, I don't feel like leaving anymore. I'll see you when you get back, sis."

"Alright."

I didn't know why she changed her mind, but I left the house. I had a missed call from the guy Jeremy from Facebook, so I decided to call him back and see what he wanted. We ended up talking until I got to my house.

As soon as I opened the door, all I heard was, "I told you I was coming for you, bitch," then I got hit with something in the back of my head.

D'Metrius

That day at the restaurant, I had to go back to the car and get my wallet. I would sometimes put it in the cupholder when I didn't feel like putting it in my pocket. Walking through the parking lot, I noticed a van driving. Maybe it was looking for a place to park. I unlocked my door and grabbed my wallet. As soon as I closed the car door, I heard a screeching sound. When I turned around to see what was going on, I got hit over my head with something, and everything went black.

When I finally woke up, I looked around, but nobody was paying attention. I noticed my wrists were tied behind my back, and I was on someone's private jet. Those niggas were playing cards and drinking. I kept my eyes closed and just listened to their conversation.

"When we get to Tampa and Dhillon gives me my payment, I'm going to Vegas to meet my shorty," one of the dudes said.

I had never seen those niggas before, but I already knew Dhillon had something to do with this. Whoever tied this knot didn't do a good job. I could easily get out of this shit. There were only three of them. One was skinny, the other one looked like he drank liquor all day, and the last one was bigger than the other two. I could take those niggas, but I didn't have a strap or anything. One thing I did that I hadn't done in a while was pray.

"Aiight, Duke, you can grab him and take him to the van. You hit his ass hard as fuck with that gun. He still knocked out, nigga"

They all laughed, and that's what I wanted them to think—I was still fucked up.

Somebody shook me and said, "Get the fuck up, nigga. We got places to be."

I moved slowly like I didn't know what was going on. There was a van outside the plane, and all three of them stood right there to make sure I got in the back. Those niggas were some goofies, but I had something in store for all of them. No one had on a mask, so I knew exactly who I was coming for after Dhillon. I had been fucking with this weak ass knot since I was on the plane. I still had my hands behind my back, though. Those fools were really bad at this shit; Dhillon should've given these niggas a test run first.

"Why wouldn't Dhillon put the plane in an area that's close to Miami? Now we still have to drive an hour with this nigga," the nigga driving complained.

"Why you keep saying his name and other information,

nigga? He is in the backseat, muthafucka!" the nigga in the passenger seat responded.

"That nigga still fucked up. Look at his ass. He ain't moved, and we only been off the plane for like forty-five minutes."

"Dhillon said he wanted him alive, bro. I hope he isn't dead. I gotta piss. I should've pissed on the damn plane," the dude in the back with me said.

"The sign said the next exit is a gas station. We'll stop there for a second, but we gotta hurry up," the driver said.

After about five minutes, I heard two doors close, and I saw some lights. I knew we were at the gas station. I peeked out of one eye and saw that the dude in the passenger seat was on his phone.

"Yeah, we got his ass. He still fucked up in the backseat."

With lightning speed, I took that rope off my wrists, then hopped up and broke this neck. I hurried up and opened the passenger door, and then I kicked his ass out that bitch. I hopped on the driver's side and took off in the van. His phone fell on the floor when I cracked his shit. I thought about picking it up, but I just waited until I saw a hotel sign and came up on the exit. Nobody checked my pockets, so I still had my wallet. I didn't know where my phone was. It probably fell in the car or around the car when that bullshit happened.

I left the van a mile before the hotel since I didn't know if it had a tracker or not. All I knew was that I needed to call my muthafuckin' people, so I walked my ass the rest of the way to the hotel. Luckily, I still had my shit wallet, so I showed him my ID, paid for the room, got my key, and went to the fourth floor. I called Wayne and told him where he could find me.

I was supposed to link up with Black's cousins when I got to Miami. I never told them to stop watching the house, so, hopefully, they would have some information when I saw them. Wayne had told me that he and our crew were already in Miami and on the way to me. I kind of figured they went looking for me because I knew Azia was going crazy.

"Bro, what the fuck happened?" Wayne walked in the door asking questions.

"I'll explain that shit later, bro. Just know that bitch ass nigga Dhillon is on some bullshit."

"What we doing, bro? Who we fucking up first?" Black asked.

"Listen, I need you to call your cousin and see what he found out. Tell him where we are, so he can meet us here."

Black pulled out his phone and made the call. "Yo, Darren, we here at the hotel. You, Diro, and Skeet, come meet us here now."

I knew we had to do something quick. Hopefully, they had guns because we didn't have anything.

"Aye, let's head to my uncle's house when they get here. I gotta let him know what's up."

"Bet, bro. We're ready for whatever, and Diro got a house full of guns. We good on that part, D. We just need a plan."

Black had just answered the question that had been on my mind for a minute.

"That's all I needed to know."

About fifteen minutes later, Darren called and said they were outside. We all left and went to my uncle's house. We were thirty minutes away. Wayne had kept all this information in his phone, including addresses and phone numbers. I called Charles to see where he was.

"What up, Unc? Where you at?"

"I went to the store. What's up, nephew?"

"I'm at your house. We need to talk."

"Alright, I'll be pulling up soon."

He didn't sound right, and something told me this was about to be some bullshit. When he pulled up, two more cars followed him into the driveway. I had my hand on the gun Diro gave me because I was ready for anything. We stepped out of both cars and stood right in the driveway.

"What's up, neph? What are you doing here?" He gave me that look I knew all too well.

"I just came to visit. You know how we do." I played it off.

"I didn't know you knew the triplets. How y'all doing, fellas?"

"You know we staying out the way," Diro said.

"Let's go in, so we can catch up," Unc said.

He walked in front of us, and I watched two men get out of both cars.

"Neph, you and your friends want a drink?"

"Yeah, get me some Henny," Punch said.

"You can give me some Patrón," Skeet responded.

The dudes with Unc kept looking at me and typing on their phones.

"You got a problem or something?" I asked.

"I'm good. I'm just playing a game on my phone," the nigga standing next to the door responded.

"Neph, they're all good people. I had to hire some security because that nigga Dhillon is sick. I know he's going to come for me next."

Boom!!

I looked around and saw people coming through the front door and the back. Everyone looked at me, and we all pulled out our guns. The security that kept looking at me started smiling, and I knew he'd set some shit up. I saw like three dudes coming in the front door and some coming in the back. My uncle went to grab his gun from under the table, and somebody shot him in the head.

"Aye, it's two on the right and three on the left."

We were deep in the living room, so they couldn't really see us, but I could see them. When they got closer, I shot one of them and had to duck behind the couch. I let off another shot, hitting another in the knee, and he fell. Shots just started ringing out, and it was about survival at that point. I was good at shooting, so those headshots came frequently.

We got outside and made it to the car. Now I was stuck

because my uncle was my only source for more information on this nigga Dhillon.

"Man, that was crazy, but it was fun." Skeet's dumb ass came running to the car, smiling.

"Nigga, that shit wasn't fun. You could've lost your fucking life," Diro said.

"But I didn't, and we're all good. Have a little fun, bro, damn."

"Nigga, stop talking to me. You're acting real childish right now."

They kept going back and forth until I turned the muthafuckin' music up on their asses. Finally, they got the hint and sat back in their seats. This shit was stressful, and I was missing my baby like crazy. I knew she was going crazy, and I really needed to talk to her.

"Aye, let me use your phone right quick," I asked Punch.

I pulled over and got out, then walked away from the car so them niggas wouldn't be in my business. Ever since she first gave it to me, I had memorized Azia's number. I called her phone, and she didn't answer until the third ring.

"Hello."

"Hey, beautiful."

"D'Metrius, is this you?"

"Yeah, baby, what are you doing? I miss you so fucking much."

"Where are you? Are you okay?"

"Yeah, I'm good, beautiful. I'm in Miami right now. I'll explain later."

"You do know your crew and your sister are coming down there to find you, right? They all left this afternoon."

"No, I didn't know Meka was coming, but I'm with the fellas right now."

"I'm mad as hell that you disappeared on me like this."

"I apologize, baby. It wasn't my fault. I promise I'll make it up to you."

"Well, while you're out there shooting your life away, think about your child too."

I looked at the phone, and she had hung up. *She didn't just basically tell me she was pregnant, did she?* I called her back three times and got the voicemail.

"Yo, man, you good?"

"Yeah, I'm good. I gotta call Meka. Azia said she left for the airport, trying to meet up with y'all."

I called Meka and told her that the fellas were with me, and she didn't have to come. She said she had missed her first flight, but she was getting on the plane, and she'd call me when she got to Miami. She hung up on me as well, and all I could do was shake my head.

We headed to another hotel closer to the city, so we could figure some shit out.

"D, we gotta get this nigga. He been doing too much lately. Maybe we can just rush in the house and start shooting any and everything walking."

Here Skeet goes with his bullshit.

"Listen, we gotta be smarter than that. We can't just rush

in and start shooting. We need to follow this nigga somewhere and get his ass," Ty suggested.

I was surprised to see him since he got shot a couple weeks ago.

"Me, personally, I want to get him by himself. All these niggas that work for him, they not really involved. He the one sending niggas our way because he's a bitch. I'll call and tell him where I am, and I'll kill myself. He fucked up when he sent those goofies to the restaurant," I said.

"If that's how you want to play it, then that's cool. Just know y'all meeting somewhere we can keep watch," Punch responded, and everyone else shook their heads in agreement.

There was a knock on the door.

"Who the hell knows we're here?" I looked at those niggas.

"Meka texted me thirty minutes ago and asked for the address. She got in an Uber," Lucus said.

I opened the door, and it was both Meka and Azia with a special guest.

Azia

"Hey, babe, I thought you could use this whore for leverage."

I walked into the room with Dhillon's daughter, figuring she'd be useful. I couldn't leave my man out in these streets, so I contacted Meka. Once she gave me the information, I called my cousin Rich and asked him for a huge favor. I also called my manager and told him I'll take the job full-time, but I needed a week before coming back. Kameila never showed back up, and I called her phone, but she didn't answer. She always got upset when I changed my mind about something. I'd give her a couple days to cool down, and then I would go and visit her with some wine and food.

"Baby, how did you get this bitch?"

"I went to the house that you told me about, and she was there, picking up a package. Since I had my gun with me, she was caught off guard and couldn't do shit. I called my cousin and asked him if his pilot could fly me here before I tracked her down. You know with my mom being a nurse, I can get some shit to knock a bitch out for some hours."

"Well, tie that bitch up to that chair in the corner, one of y'all," Metri said.

I was at the right place at the right time because I caught this bitch right when she ran up on the porch to get that package. Her car was still running with the music blasting. I snuck up on her, put my gun in her back, and told her that I would put a bullet in her head if she did anything. I lied, though. I had never shot anyone in my life. The only time I had fired a gun was when D'Metrius taught me a month ago.

Lucus took the chick and tied her to a chair with a cord. The guys were discussing how they wanted to leave at midnight to see what was going on at Dhillon's house. Meka and I stayed behind with this Hershey chick, and I decided to have a little fun with her.

"You know my daddy is going to kill all y'all mutha-fuckas!" she yelled.

"Yeah, well, we'll take you with us, bitch," I said.

"Your daddy is a pussy. He got all these men doing his dirty work. You're a runner, so shut the fuck up before I slap yo' ass." Meka went straight in!

"Fuck you, bitch. If I wasn't tied to this chair, I'd whoop your ass." Hershey tried to spit on Meka, and she slapped her ass hard as fuck.

"Did you check her for any trackers? They always have some type of tracker." Meka asked me.

"No, I didn't think about that."

I stood there with the gun pointed at Hershey's head while Meka searched her. She checked to see if she had any jewelry on, then patted her down to see if she could find anything, but she found nothing.

As Meka checked Hershey, I saw her clenching her legs real close together.

"Check her ankles, Mek."

When Meka patted her right ankle and lifted her pant leg, we saw an anklet, and it was blinking. I got terrified because someone could be tracking her at that moment.

Meka ripped the tracker off Hershey's leg and threw it in the toilet. I called D'Metrius and didn't get an answer. She called Lucus, and the same thing happened.

"Nobody is fucking answering, and I'm getting irritated. Somebody could be looking for her, Meka." I had to whisper because I didn't want Hershey to hear what we were saying. She did not need to know that I was having a mini panic attack.

Meka had tried calling Wayne and Lucus again and got the same thing. I couldn't understand this shit. I had just gotten off the phone with D'Metrius not too long ago, so I didn't know why he wasn't answering.

"We can leave her here and get out now before anybody shows up," I suggested.

"What would be the point of leverage if we leave her here?" Meka countered.

"I don't know. I'm just trying to come up with something since we only have two guns."

"It'll be fine. If someone was coming for her, trust me, they would've been here by now."

Meka was right. It had been about an hour since the fellas left us. I didn't even know how I ended up in this position again, but I felt like I loved this nigga, and I couldn't let anything happen to him. I would've regretted not coming if something happened. Hershey looked like she was asleep, so I walked over to make sure.

"You know my tracker is waterproof." She smiled.

"Bitch, fuck you and yo' tracker. If somebody was coming—"

That's all I could get out before the room door flew open, and three men came in with guns pointed at us. We pulled out our weapons too. I had mine pointed at this bitch in the chair while Meka had hers pointed at them.

"Give us the girl, and we won't shoot you," one of the men said.

"I'll shoot this bitch before you take her," I responded like I was about this life.

"This is the last time I'm saying it. Give me the girl."

"No, sir, I can't do that. We need her, so you can tell your master that," Meka said.

Pow!

I looked around, and Meka had shot one of the dudes in

the knee. The other two tried to rush me but ended up shooting the bitch in the chair. I ran to Meka and told her, let's go. Before we could open the door, shots rang out again. People were running out of their rooms to see what was going on. We ran down two flights of stairs until we got to the back door.

"Somebody has to answer their phone! I don't know what to do, and I know they're still coming after us," I cried.

"Yeah, Azia, I'm scared too."

We finally made it to the car. I was wondering where the hell we were about to go. Before I could even get a word out, both windows shattered, and arms were reaching into the car, trying to open the door.

"Meka, start the car and pull off!" I screamed.

I couldn't find my gun. I think I dropped it while running out of the hotel. Meka pulled off with one guy's arm still in the window.

"It's a truck back there following us. Make a left," I said with panic in my voice.

"Girl, why these niggas haven't answered the phone or even called us?" Meka shouted.

"At this point, I just want to go back home. I don't know why I even came here."

"Listen, Azia, I know why you came here. You wanted to help your man. I wanted to help my brothers, but I'm scared too. To tell you the truth, I have never done anything like this before. I have shot my gun a couple times, but that's it. I don't know where we're going right now, and I'm tempted to just head to the airport."

I should've followed my first thought and stayed at home. I always tell people to follow their first thought because that second thought could fuck you up. Look at my situation. I was stuck driving around in a car with two broken windows and the bumper hanging off, and none of the guys were answering their phones. This was some bullshit.

"Well, I'm with whatever you plan on doing."

BOOM!

That was all we heard before the car went off the road and flipped onto the freeway.

Kameila

 had been tied to a chair for two days. When I walked through the door of my home, I was hit in the head with a bat. The next thing I remembered was waking up in a chair with two dudes standing on the wall, watching me. I asked them who they were and why they were there, but I didn't get an answer. I had a gun under my table, and I needed to get to it.

"Why am I tied to this chair?" I asked.

"You'll find out in a minute," one of the dudes finally answered.

"Why can't I find out now? What the hell y'all want?"

I heard some heels clicking on my kitchen floor, and as I turned my head, this bitch Rosalina walked in. She was smiling while smoking a blunt. Then she walked around the chair and blew smoke in my face. If I wasn't tied up, I would've beaten her ass again.

"You're a feisty little one. I see why my baby daddy likes you."

"Cut to the chase. What the fuck do you want?"

"I want you dead, but before that happens, I need some information."

"Information? Bitch, I don't have any information."

"Keep cussing at me, and I'm gon' slap you."

"Just because you got me tied up doesn't mean I can't speak my mind. If you gon' kill me, then do that, bitch."

Slap!

"See, I just told you about your mouth. Now, watch it, bitch. Where is my baby daddy and my son?"

This bitch was going to die by my hands. She had me fucked up, and I wasn't telling her shit. The two dudes walked away when she came into the living room. I didn't know why this bitch kept playing with me. Wayne didn't want her, and she needed to get that through her head.

"I don't know where your baby daddy is or your son."

Slap!

"Bitch, quit playing with me. I know you know where he's at."

"I don't know where your family is. I haven't spoken to Wayne in a month."

"You really want me to believe that?"

"I really don't care what you believe at this point. Can you just kill me or let me go?"

She walked away, and the two guys came back and stood back in their places. I heard my back door close, and I knew she had left. I had a window in my bathroom downstairs, and I was about to jump out of it. I just needed to grab the spare keys to the car, and they were hanging on the kitchen wall.

"Can I use the bathroom, please?"

"We let you go yesterday."

"Today is a whole new day, and I have to shit, so can I please go to the bathroom? Unless you want me to do it right here."

"Listen, don't take a long time."

He untied the rope, and I stretched first, trying to stall. The other guy's phone rang, and he walked outside. I decided to walk to the kitchen and sneak the keys into my bra. The keys were on the wall, so as long as I didn't mess up, it should be good.

"Why are you walking so slow? You need me to carry you?"

"You wish. Homeboy, I'm trying to get the feeling back in my body, sir. I have been tied up in a chair for two days."

"Yeah, well, tell the lady where her son is, and you can have your house back."

"I don't fucking know where he's at like I told her goofy ass."

I kept walking, running my right hand against the wall, and grabbed the key with no problem. I only responded to stall for more time. When I saw the other guy come back in, I went into the bathroom. He needed to be back in the house, so he wouldn't see me crawling to my car. I had some

Pine-Sol in the bathroom cabinet, so I opened it and put it under the toilet seat in case one of them was standing by the door listening.

As the Pine-Sol poured into the toilet, I lifted the window, hopped on the ledge, and jumped to the ground. I crawled all the way to my car, got in on the passenger side, and quickly got in the driver's seat.

I started the car and peeled out of the driveway, driving fast as hell to Azia's house. Her car wasn't there, so I went to her mother's house.

"Hey, Ms. Cook, have you talked to Azia?"

"No, baby, I haven't. Is everything okay with you?"

"No. Can I please come in?"

"Of course. I'll get you something to slip on, and you can take a shower. We can talk about what's going on after you're done."

"Thank you so much."

I walked upstairs and started the shower. Man, I was so furious with this bitch. The dummies she had watching me didn't even know I left the house. That's how stupid they were. I had on some leggings, and I was switching this ass while walking to the bathroom. I knew ole boy who was talking shit was staring, so I did it ten times harder than usual.

"Kameila, are you okay, honey?" Ms. Cook asked.

"No. Wayne's baby mother broke into my house and held me for two days. She thinks I know where her son is," I told her.

"Wayne is the guy that be hanging with Azia's friend?"

"Yes. How long has it been since you spoke with her? I rode past her house, and her car wasn't there."

"I think it's been about two days now. I called her earlier, but she didn't answer."

"Oh no, oh no, oh nooo."

I started thinking really hard about where Azia could be. With all this stuff going on, she could've been anywhere. I took out my phone and checked her Facebook page, but nothing was on there. Ms. Cook had made some tea, and I was drinking it like it was water. I was trying not to have a panic attack because I didn't need her freaking out.

"Why are you saying oh no? Kameila, what's wrong?"

"I don't know what's going on right now, but it can't be good. I don't want you to panic, but I think she's been kidnapped by some people who want D'Metrius dead."

"We need to call the police right now." She reached for her phone.

"Wait! We can't call them yet," I said.

She got out of the chair and started pacing the floor. I rubbed my hand across my face. This was stressful, and I was about to call Wayne and see if he knew anything.

"Hey, Wayne, this is Kameila. Can you please call me back?"

I had to leave a voicemail because he didn't answer. When I called Meka, she didn't answer either. So, I decided to go to Azia's house again.

"Do you have a spare key to Azia's house?" I asked Ms. Cook.

"Yes, I do. Are we going over there?"

"Yes, we need to see what's going on."

Ms. Cook slipped on some sandals and grabbed her purse, then we were out the door. As we drove through traffic, she started praying, and I prayed with her. When we pulled up to Azia's house, her car still wasn't there. We got out and looked around, but no one was outside, and nothing looked different, so we walked up to the door and unlocked it.

"Her house still looks the same. Nothing is out of place," I said.

"I'll check around upstairs. If she's not there, then we're going to her job."

"I'll check the basement."

As I walked down the stairs, I started to panic. My mom used to lock me in the basement for two hours whenever she would get upset and couldn't have her way with something. She would hate it when I came back from my dad's house with new things, so that was my punishment for about two years.

"Nothing is wrong in the basement. Did you find anything upstairs?"

"No, everything looks good."

Ms. Cook hung her head and walked toward the door, and I followed. We were going to the airport to see if Azia had gone to work and was on the plane.

When we got to the airport, we walked up to the booth where the planes loaded and spoke to a lady.

"Hello, how may I help you today?"

"I need to speak to the supervisor of the flight attendants," I said.

"I'll page Mr. Jones for you right away."

A minute later, a man walked out the door behind the lady who had just helped us. I shook his hand, and Ms. Cook started asking questions.

"I'm looking for my daughter, Azia Cook. I wanted to know if anyone has seen her. I have a feeling she's been kidnapped."

"I haven't seen her today, but I talked to her yesterday. She called and told me that she'll accept the job full-time, but she needed a week to come back. I hope nothing bad has happened to her."

I know her ass didn't go to Miami, I thought. But I wasn't gonna say anything because her mother was already panicking. When Mr. Jones said a week for her to come back, I knew it was more to the story, and she was not kidnapped. We thanked him and left to head back to Azia's house.

Wayne

We drove thirty-five minutes to get to the storage place. When we got to the gate, a man was standing there, asking for ID. I told him we were coming to pick something up for my uncle. He was acting like an ass, and I was ready to run this nigga over.

"Listen, we're picking up something for my uncle. We won't be long. You can follow us."

"I can't follow you because I'm the only one here."

I pulled out my gun. "You either gon' let us in here or lose your life over a fucking a job that pays you nine dollars an hour."

The guard started shaking and looking around. When my eyes followed his, I saw that he was looking at a camera. I got out of the truck with my ski mask pulled down and shot that bitch out. At that point, I was quite sure he had pissed himself.

"Last time," D said.

"Alright, you guys can go through."

"Give me your cell phone."

"I need this. I have a pregnant wife at home, and she calls me every hour," he stuttered.

"We'll drop it back off when we leave, nigga. Now give it here."

He wasn't gon' survive, and I believed he was lying about his wife. We drove through and rushed to find the door. I knew there had to be a phone in the booth that he was in, so we had to move fast. After going around two corners, we saw the number 704. Just what we were looking for.

"D, hurry up, bro. I think that lame ass nigga called the police," I said.

D jumped out of the truck and went to unlock the door. He didn't know which key it was, so he tried damn near all of them. He finally got it open, and there was a big white van parked in the storage unit.

"Start that bitch up, and let's go," I said.

As we pulled out, I stopped by the gate where the guard was and threw his phone out the window. Just as we were leaving the lot, I saw two police cars approaching the entrance with their sirens on. I knew that bitch ass nigga had called the police when we went to the back. I should've just shot his ass and left it at that.

"Bro, these two police cars are behind me. I'm about to lose their ass. Go back toward the hotel," D called me and said.

"Nigga, we following you. Now, drive!"

Before I could hang up the phone good, that fool flew past us fast as hell in that damn kidnapper van. The two police cars sped up, and I was right behind them. Meka kept blowing my phone up, but I couldn't answer; I had to concentrate. When I looked in the rearview mirror, there were two police cars behind me. I had to lose their ass. I made a right and got on the freeway. I wasn't even following D anymore; I had to lose those fools. Speeding in and out of traffic, I didn't know where I would end up, but I wasn't stopping until I had to.

"Come up on this exit and make a left," Black said.

"Nigga, how you know where to go?"

"Nigga my family is in this truck. Plus, I been here plenty of times. So I know where the fuck I'm going."

"Turn down that alley and park under the tent," Darren interrupted his response.

"Nigga, I'm not parking nowhere. How do you know them damn cops aren't coming up the street?"

"If you park and cut the lights out, trust me, no one is coming back here. If they do, we shoot their ass."

I really didn't have anywhere to go, so parking was the only option before we ran out of gas. I called D's phone, but I didn't get an answer, so I called Lucus. He said they lost the cops and asked where we were.

"D about to pull up," I said.

He pulled up in like two minutes, and we started

packing the guns in the back of the truck. Then we pulled off, headed to Dhillon's house.

"Aye, you talked to the girls?" D asked me.

"Naw, Meka called me, but I was driving, so I couldn't answer."

"She called me too and Azia, but my phone was on the floor."

"Lucus, you talked to my sister?" D asked.

"I just heard her message. She said some guys came to the hotel, and they had a shootout. They don't know where to go, and the girl is dead."

"What the fuck? How did they know what hotel we were at?"

"I don't know, bro, but that's what she left on the voicemail."

D sat in the passenger seat and rubbed his hand down his face. I knew he was stressed about all this shit. His uncle had gotten shot in the midst of everything, two of his partners got kidnapped, and them niggas were probably dead by now. We were about five minutes away from the hotel when we got detoured because of an accident.

"Let's head to the room and get the ladies. We can go straight to Dhillon's house after we grab them."

"Call Azia and tell her to come outside. We are one minute away," I told D.

He called Azia and didn't get an answer, then he called Meka, and the same thing happened. D and I were about to go up to the room when we saw four police cars. We didn't know what was going on, so we decided to try it anyway.

"Excuse me, sir. You can't go up there."

"Why? My room is on the second floor, and my things are in there."

"Sir, there has been a shooting, and this is an active crime scene. I apologize about your things. If you leave your number, I can call you when everything is over."

All I heard was *shooting*, and my mind went blank. D was calling the girls back-to-back but wasn't getting an answer. I was terrified, and I hoped nothing had happened to them. I left her my number, and we went back outside. There were more police cars out there, and I needed to find out what was going on.

"I'm about to ask this officer what happened and see if she tells me anything different," I told D.

"Bro, be careful, and take that strap off your hip."

I walked over to the lady cop who was writing on her notepad. She was thick and looked damn good in that uniform. I decided to use my charm and see if she'd give me the answers I needed.

"Excuse me, my sister is staying at this hotel, and I can't go up to check on her. Can you tell me what happened?"

"Yes, there is a dead body upstairs, and we're trying to figure out what's going on. Have you seen or heard anything?"

"No, ma'am, I haven't. Thank you for the information."

"Here's my card. Call me if you hear something."

"Sure, or I'll just call you when I want to hear that sexy voice."

"I like that even better."

She turned around and walked back to the door. As I walked, I saw a lot of glass in this one particular parking spot. I walked over there, and it looked like glass from a car window. I didn't know how the lady cop didn't see it.

"Yo, she just told me it's a dead body upstairs and asked if I knew anything," I told D when I got back to the car.

"A dead body, what the fuck? And I've still been calling the girls and haven't gotten an answer."

"Look, they did say Hershey was dead. I also saw some glass in the parking space over there. It looks like glass from a car window."

"Lucus, don't you still have that tracker on your phone for Meka?"

"Yeah, hold on."

I had to pull off because we didn't want the police coming over and asking questions. Later, I would call that cop and see if she'd tell me anything else. I had a really strange feeling that this had something to do with Dhillon all over again.

"I bet you this got something to with Dhillon. Man, I'm sick of this nigga. Let's head over there." D said the same shit I was thinking.

"You just said what I was thinking. Let's go."

We rode past that accident again, but they were clearing it out. I didn't see any cars, so they must've towed them.

"Everybody strap up because we're going in, guns blazing. Fuck these niggas!" I said to everyone.

"You know we're ready, bro," Ty said.

D'Metrius

 an, I can't get a break. I hoped and prayed that Azia and Meka were okay. I didn't know why they weren't answering their phones, but it had me buggin'.

"Aye, D, my mom just called me in a panic saying she was watching the news, and that accident we saw on the freeway had two females in one car and three dudes in a truck," Darren said.

"Man, I hope that's not them. Did they transport them to a hospital? I'll go check because I need answers at this point."

"She didn't say."

"We have to start with the closest hospital and go from there."

I googled the closest hospital, and it was ten minutes away. As we drove, I prayed it wasn't them. I had just lost my mother, and I wouldn't be able to take it if I lost my sister and my girl too. Before Wayne could come to a complete stop, I jumped out and went into the hospital. There was a lady standing at the counter, playing with her fingernails, and I cleared my throat.

"Hello, sir, can I help you with something?"

"Yes, can you tell me if you have two girls in this hospital who were in a car accident like an hour ago?"

"What's the name of the patients, sir?"

"D'Meka Mags and Azia Cook."

"Hold on one second."

I stood there, tapping my foot on the floor and rubbing my hands together.

"We do have two ladies here from a car accident, but they're listed as Jane Doe."

"Can I look and see if they're my people, please?"

"I'm sorry. I can't do that, sir."

"Well, let me talk to the manager."

She called the manager over the phone and said she'd be down in five minutes. I was tripping hard as hell because I just had this feeling.

"Hello, sir, how may I help you?"

"Me and my family came here for a vacation. When I got back to the hotel, my sister and my girlfriend weren't there. I heard about this accident with two females, and I just want to know if it's them."

"I'm not supposed to do this, but since you're on vacation, I'll help you out. I'm only letting you in one room, sir."

"Okay, that's fine. Thank you."

If one of them was Meka or Azia, then they both were there. I walked behind her as she pushed for the elevator. We went up four floors, made a right, and stopped in front of an open door. There was a body under some covers. As I walked up closer, I could see the braids that my sister had. My eyes watered when I saw tubes in her nose and down her throat.

"Can you have the doctor come in here and tell me what happened to my sister?"

"Yes, but can you tell me some more information please, and I'll have her come down right away, sir."

She asked me her age, where we were from, and if she had any health conditions. After she paged the doctor, the lady left the room. I sat there and just stared at Meka. She looked like she was peaceful, but I couldn't stand to see her like that: breathing machines, an IV in her hand, and a cast on her leg. I knew my mama was probably cussing me out right now.

"Hello, sir, I'm Doctor Miles. Is this your sister?"

"Yes, it is. Can you tell me what happened?"

"I don't know the full story, but I do know that she was brought in because her car flipped onto the freeway. It landed on the passenger side. I put her in a medically induced coma to help with the swelling in her brain. Her right leg is broken also."

"The other lady in the car is my girlfriend. Can I see her?"

"I can't right now. She had to get emergency surgery, and she's in the ICU."

"Is that all you can tell me?"

"That's all the information I have right now. I'll keep you updated. Leave me your name and number, and I'll contact you soon. Your sister can hear you if you want to talk to her,"

I gave her my number, then sat back in the chair and pulled out my phone. I called Punch and told him the news. He was walking into the hospital, so I gave him the room number.

"Damn, bro, this fucked up," Punch said when he walked in.

"Man, this shit is crazy as hell. The doctor said the car flipped onto the freeway and landed on the passenger side. I'm quite sure Meka was driving, so that means it landed on Azia's side."

"Damn, man, I don't even know what to say, but I told the fellas to find another hotel and lay low for the night. Ty is gonna call me when they make it."

"I was surprised to see him here."

"You know I was keeping his ass in the loop, and when I told him you went missing, he was like, 'come pick me up. I want to help y'all find my brother.'"

"If I don't know nothing else, I know y'all two niggas got my back through whatever."

"All day, bro."

We sat in silence for a few minutes as we waited for the

doctor to come back in. I was thinking about calling Azia's mom and letting her know what happened. The only thing is, I didn't have her phone number, but Punch could call Kameila and let her know.

"Yo, call Kameila and let her know what's going on, so she can give the info to Ms. Cook."

"Alright, bro, I got you."

He placed the call and put it on speaker. When Kameila answered, she sounded upset.

"Wayne, why haven't you been answering my calls? I've called you four times."

"Listen, shorty, I didn't get a call from you. I need you to sit down, so I can talk to you."

"I am sitting down with Ms. Cook. We're looking for Azia."

When she said that, I hung my head.

"She's in Miami, and she's been in an accident. Y'all need to get here as soon as possible."

All I heard was Ms. Cook screaming and Kameila asking more questions. He told her what we knew, and they said they were getting on the next flight. I felt terrible for having to deliver some news like that to a parent.

"I'm about to go to the vending machine. You want something, bro?" I asked Punch.

"Bring me some water and some chips. I haven't ate shit all day."

It was one o'clock in the morning, and I was tired as hell, but I refused to leave my sister's side. Walking to the vending machine, I saw a guy dressed in all black. I didn't trust anybody wearing all black with all this shit going on, so I slowly walked past, so I could listen to what he was saying.

"My sister was in a car accident, and I wanted to check on her."

"Follow me, sir."

He followed her, and I followed closely behind them. The only person who would want to check on an accident while wearing all black, looking like a security guard, was Dhillon's people. The vending machine could wait. She took him to a room on the corner and left him. I was still standing there, looking at his ass. He was up to something, and I wanted to know what it was. The nigga walked into the room and looked around to make sure nobody was looking. He walked by the tubes and was about to press a button when I walked into the room.

"What the fuck are you doing?"

"Who the fuck are you?"

"That doesn't matter. Why are you in this room?"

"You the hospital police, muthafucka?

I stared at his ass for a minute because I knew that deep ass voice. Then a picture popped into my head. I knew who he was when I saw that big slash across his right eye. He was Dhillon's right-hand man.

"Nigga, you know who I am. You thought you was slick with that hat on, tryna cover that eye. I don't forget faces."

He started walking up, and since I didn't get checked at the door, I still had my pistol on me.

"Bitch ass nigga, you want to die here, or you want to get the fuck out now?"

"Nigga, you in a hospital. You ain't about to use that gun."

I had a silencer, so I shot his ass in both legs and walked out the door. That wasn't even Azia's room; I just knew he was being sneaky. I heard him screaming for help, so I hopped on the elevator and went to the cafeteria.

Kameila

Once I got that call, we left Azia's house and went straight to the airport. I couldn't believe the news I had just heard. Ms. Cook was crying her eyes out, and I was trying to be strong while shedding tears here and there. I had to keep her calm and let her know everything would be just fine. Although I told her that, I still prayed for my girl. I went to work yesterday and couldn't really focus because I had been thinking about Azia since I left her house that night. I hoped my friend would be alright and that her injuries were minor.

"We need two seats on the next flight to Miami," I said to the reservations agent at the airline counter.

"Let me check and see if we have some available." She typed a few strokes on her computer. "Uhh, I have only one ticket available for the last flight today. It leaves in an hour."

I looked at Ms. Cook. She was so upset, and I was too.

The best thing would be for her to take the seat and go to Miami, so she could get to the hospital. I would catch the next flight tomorrow morning, and that would give me some time to get things in order with my job. Before I knew it, Ms. Cook was asking people if they had a flight to Miami and offering to pay them double for their ticket.

"Nobody wants to sell their ticket," she said.

"It's okay, Ms. Cook. I'll just catch a flight tomorrow morning. Give me your phone, so I can put Wayne's number in. When you land, he'll be right there waiting for you, and he'll get you straight to the hospital."

"Okay. I really appreciate you, Kameila. Thank you."

"You're welcome, Ms. Cook. Have a safe flight."

She went through the check-in, and I went back to my car. I called Wayne and told him that Ms. Cook would be at the airport in Miami soon and to pick her up. I felt so bad; I should've stayed at Azia's house that night. Neither of us would be going through what we're going through if I had.

I drove back home and packed my things since I had decided to stay at a hotel. With everything going on, I just needed a drink and some sleep. Before I left home, I ordered my ticket online, and I would be on the first flight in the morning.

"Hello, welcome to the Holiday Inn. How may I assist you?" the front desk clerk said when I walked into the hotel.

"I just need a one-bedroom with a Jacuzzi for one night."

"We have one available for you. How would you like to pay?"

"Credit card." I handed her my ID and American Express.

"Okay, you're all set."

I went to the elevator and took it to the fifth floor. My room was three doors down. When I opened the door, I threw my bag on the floor and went straight to the mini-fridge. It was stocked with all kinds of liquor and juices. I even had a kitchen, but I wouldn't need to use that because I would only be there for a couple of hours. It was already eleven at night.

After I got in the shower, I put on my swimsuit, started the Jacuzzi, and made myself a Hennessy and cranberry juice. I turned the TV on and sat in the Jacuzzi, scrolling through my phone. There was a party going on tonight, and I wished I could go. I needed some peace and some fun.

Just as I started to relax, there was a knock at the door.

Now, who the fuck is at this door? Nobody knows I'm here!

When I peeked out the peephole and didn't see anyone, I turned the TV down and grabbed my gun out of my bag. Then I turned the lights off and just listened to see if I could hear anything. I kept sipping on my liquor, thinking my mind was playing tricks on me. After a few minutes, I didn't hear anything. *Maybe the knock came from the TV,* I thought. Since I was starving, I decided to call for room service.

"Yes, I would like to order some chicken wings and fries."

"Will that be all, ma'am?"

"Yes, that'll be all. How long will it take?"

"About twenty minutes, ma'am."

"Okay, thank you."

I went to the bathroom and turned the shower on, then I went to the bedroom and grabbed my toothbrush and some underwear. By the time I got out of the shower, my food should be coming, and Ms. Cook's flight will have landed. This shower felt so good. I had been with Ms. Cook at Azia's house, trying to figure things out, and my body was a ball of stress.

"Hey, Wayne, did you pick up Ms. Cook yet?"

"Yeah, she landed. We're on the way to the hospital now."

"I'm glad she made it safely. Can you keep me updated on what's going on? I'll be on the plane in the morning. They only had one ticket for the flight that left today."

"Alright, sounds good. Make sure you call me, and I'll come get you from the airport."

"I sure will. Keep me posted, and I'll talk to you tomorrow."

I hung up and put on my underwear, then covered myself with a robe that was in the bathroom. Once I was settled, I made another drink and finished watching TV. When I called room service to see what was taking so long, they said they didn't have an order from my room.

"Sir, I just called and made an order. They said it would be up in twenty minutes."

"I apologize, ma'am. I can put your order in and have it for you right away."

"This doesn't make any sense. Can you just send me some chicken wings, please?"

"Yes, ma'am. I'll have it up right away."

That was so crazy to me. I had literally just called and talked to someone. I guess I didn't have a choice but to wait until it arrived. Fifteen minutes passed, and I finally heard a knock on the door. I jumped up. I was so hungry, and drinking this liquor didn't do anything to help.

"Room service," I heard them yell and knock again.

I opened the door, and before I could grab the food, I was hit in the head. I fell to the floor and started screaming. The person dragged me back to the bedroom and closed the door.

"Help! What do you want from me?" I yelled as I struggled to get free.

Silence.

"Why are you doing this to me?"

Silence.

"Who are you?"

Silence.

I couldn't believe this was happening again.

"Hello, Kameila, I'm Dhillon. I'm sure you know your little boyfriend has a debt that he hasn't paid yet. Him and his little homies think I don't know that they're in Miami, trying to kill me."

"Listen, I have nothing to do with this."

"Would you like to die now or later?"

"I... I don't want to die at all."

"If you can get your little boyfriend to come back here alone, I'll pay you fifty thousand dollars, but he's more than likely going to die. The choice is yours, and you have ten minutes to decide." He put the bag of money on the bed.

What the fuck? I needed the money, and I didn't want to die, but damn. I didn't want Wayne to die either!

To be continued!!!

CPSIA information can be obtained
at www.ICGtesting.com
Printed in the USA
LVHW030746100921
697444LV00005B/327

9 781648 543708